"Who would want to hurt you?"

When Lindy whirled and gawked at him, Thad was certain he'd asked the right question. "What do you mean, hurt me?"

"Just what I said. This is no computer mix-up. It's deliberate. Somebody wants you broke and they've just about succeeded in making that happen. What I need to know is, why? Who's that mad at you, Lindy?"

"Nobody." She leaned her elbows on her knees and cupped her face in her hands.

"Okay," he drawled, choosing his words carefully, "then who might still have it in for your late husband?"

Her head snapped up. Her jaw gaped. It took several long seconds for her to regain her composure and in that short space of time Thad saw a myriad of conflicting emotions.

"You don't have to tell me a thing," Thad said. "But you should confide in someone, preferably somebody in law enforcement. You do see that, don't you?"

She pulled her jacket tighter. "I...can't."

He had to find out why.

Books by Valerie Hansen

Love Inspired Suspense

*Her Brother's Keeper
*Out of the Depths
  Deadly Payoff
*Shadow of Turning
  Hidden in the Wall
*Nowhere to Run
*No Alibi
*My Deadly Valentine
    "Dangerous Admirer"
  Face of Danger
†Nightwatch
  The Rookie's Assignment
†Threat of Darkness
†Standing Guard

Love Inspired Historical

  Frontier Courtship
  Wilderness Courtship
  High Plains Bride
  The Doctor's Newfound Family
  Rescuing the Heiress

Love Inspired

*The Perfect Couple
*Second Chances
*Love One Another
*Blessings of the Heart
*Samantha's Gift
*Everlasting Love
  The Hamilton Heir
*A Treasure of the Heart
  Healing the Boss's Heart

*Serenity, Arkansas
†The Defenders

VALERIE HANSEN

was thirty when she awoke to the presence of the Lord in her life and turned to Jesus. In the years that followed, she worked with young children, both in church and secular environments. She also raised a family of her own and played foster mother to a wide assortment of furred and feathered critters.

Married to her high school sweetheart, she now lives in an old farmhouse she and her husband renovated with their own hands. She loves to hike the wooded hills behind the house and reflect on the marvelous turn her life has taken. Not only is she privileged to reside among the loving, accepting folks in the breathtakingly beautiful Ozark mountains of Arkansas, she also gets to share her personal faith by telling the stories of her heart for all of the Love Inspired Books lines.

Life doesn't get much better than that!

STANDING
GUARD

VALERIE HANSEN

Love Inspired

™ LOVE INSPIRED BOOKS

ISBN-13: 978-0-373-67526-5

STANDING GUARD

Copyright © 2012 by Valerie Whisenand

www.LoveInspiredBooks.com

Printed in U.S.A.

Yea, though I walk through the valley of the shadow of death, I will fear no evil; for thou art with me; thy rod and thy staff they comfort me.
—*Psalms* 23:4

I wish I could honor all the people, past and present, who have brought me to the place in my life, and in my faith, where I'm able to write these stories. There would not be room for all those names if I took up pages and pages, so I'll simply say a heartfelt "Thank you" to friends and family.

ONE

"Mama? Mama?"

The little voice was barely audible, yet it was enough to reach into Lindy Southerland's subconscious and rouse her from a troubled sleep.

She sat up in bed, raked her long, reddish-gold hair back with her fingers and strained to listen. Could she have imagined hearing Danny calling?

Suddenly, something hit the floor somewhere in the otherwise silent house. The thud was muted but unmistakable. Had her only child fallen out of bed?

"Mama?"

Danny's high-pitched plea was tinged with anxiety. "Coming, honey," she called. She hadn't imagined hearing it the first time. Poor little guy sounded scared. Again. No wonder. Neither of them had slept well since they'd seen Ben...

Banishing the memories of her family's kidnapping and her husband's murder that continued to haunt her, Lindy threw back her blankets, stood to slip into a warm robe and belted it, while exiting her room.

How she hated the night. Her irrational fears had increased in the six months since she'd been tragically widowed and she didn't know how to fight back. Or how to help her seven-year-old son.

She took a settling breath and mustered her courage. Danny needed her. That was all that mattered.

"It's okay," she whispered, trying to fool herself by pretending she was composed and unruffled. "I'm okay. Danny's okay. We're fine now."

But she wasn't fine. And her little boy wasn't fine, either. They'd been through too much, seen too much, suffered too much.

"I'm coming, honey," she repeated. "Mama's coming."

Trembling inside, she padded barefoot down the second floor hallway. Danny's open door was illuminated by one of the tiny night-lights she had placed throughout the house after her son had begged for them. Not that she blamed him. Their world seemed far less gloomy and intimidating when it wasn't filled with darkness.

Lindy expected to spot his tousled head on the pillow but the blankets were too bunched.

She tiptoed closer.

Reached for the edge of the covers.

"Mama!"

Lindy whirled in the direction of the distant echo. He sounded *terrified!*

Without pausing to think, she physically answered the child's summons, her feet slapping the cold, hardwood floor, the hem of her robe fluttering behind her as she bounded down the stairs as fast as she could without falling.

She paused at the bottom. "Danny? Where are you?"

All she could hear was his whimpering nearby. Had he been sleepwalking and awakened somewhere other than his bed? That was most likely the case. It had happened before. The pediatrician had assured her it was probably just a phase the child was going through but that didn't keep Lindy from hurting for her confused little boy.

"Danny?" Still on the trail of his soft sobbing, she dashed past the entrance to the ultramodern kitchen.

What she glimpsed in her peripheral vision took a second to register. Although momentum had already carried her well beyond the doorway, she suddenly realized she'd seen movement. Menace.

A huge, dark shape jerked and shifted as she darted past.

Lindy almost faltered. If not for the continuing sounds of her child's weeping she might have bolted, run for her life. But she could not think only of herself. She had to find Danny.

She rounded the corner into the living room and stopped. Held her breath. Cast around with her eyes and saw no one. Nothing. Where *was* he? His last plea had definitely come from this direction but there was no sign of him now.

The sound of childish crying had ceased. All she could hear now was muttered cursing and multiple, heavy footsteps behind her. There had to be at least two prowlers, maybe more, and she had nowhere else to go. She was cornered!

The high back of the brown tweed sofa caught her eye. It wasn't much but it was the only object in the room big enough to provide an adequate hiding place. She prayed Danny was safe, well hidden.

Lindy raced for cover, turned sideways, edged behind the bulky piece of furniture and then froze momentarily, straining to listen, to better assess her situation.

A shout of, "Get her," made the fine hairs on her arms prickle more than the icy February weather outside.

"Why me?" another male voice replied. "You're the clumsy one. We could of gotten in and out without a problem if you hadn't dropped that stuff."

"Shut up and do as you're told. I'm almost done."

Lindy nearly gasped aloud when something cold touched her ankle.

"Mama?"

She fell to her knees, opened her arms and pulled the thin figure closer. "Danny!" His name was little more than a hint on her breath.

"Mama, I…"

"Hush." Lindy gathered his shivering body closer. "Don't talk."

A nod told her that he understood. Satisfied, she grasped his shoulders and held him so they were eye to eye. Terror painted his shadowy expression so vividly Lindy could hardly bear to look.

"Shush," she mouthed, directing the boy's attention beyond their hiding place with nothing more than rapid eye movement. They could hear at least one person drawing nearer. Once the footfalls reached the carpeted living room, however, the noise was muted.

They heard that prowler pause and yell to his partner. "I don't see 'em in here."

Lindy pulled closer her quivering child and held tight. Was it possible this man was too dumb to think of looking behind the couch? Could anyone be that dense?

A long shadow flowed across the floor and crept up the wall behind her. He might be slow-witted but he was coming closer just the same. Should they stay there like sitting ducks or make a run for it?

Was there a chance they could get to the front

door, unlock it and flee before he overtook them? She doubted it. Besides, it was freezing outside and Danny was wearing only light flannel pajamas.

"I'm done in here," the more distant prowler shouted. "C'mon. Let's go."

"You sure? What if she saw us?" The bulky shadow shifted and shortened slightly, as if the man might be moving away.

"What do you care? You know what happens to witnesses who get in our way."

The man closest to Lindy laughed hoarsely, making her skin crawl. She bit her lip to stifle the urge to scream.

"Yeah," he said, projecting his voice as if making an announcement. "No cops, lady. You got that? You rat to the police and we'll be back. Next time, you and your brat won't be as lucky as you were when good old Ben got what was coming to him."

He was still snorting and chuckling as the sound of his morbid attempt at humor faded away.

Lindy slumped down, pulled Danny into her lap and just sat there, rocking him and weeping silent tears while she wondered what to do next. She knew she should call the sheriff and report the break-in. That's what a normal person would do.

But she wasn't a normal person, she was the widow of Ben Southerland. And Danny was his son. Some of the higher-ups in the criminal organization that had abducted her and Danny, and had cost Ben his life when he'd tried to save them, had evaded capture.

The police had assured her that those kinds of white-collar crooks would have no further interest in her family.

Lindy had wanted desperately to trust their opinion and had almost convinced herself they were right—until tonight.

Thad Pearson wasn't trying to eavesdrop on the women's conversation. He was simply standing in line several places behind them while waiting to order his fast food lunch at Hickory Station before returning to work at Pearson Products. The fact that one of them was Samantha Rochard Waltham, a former nemesis of his in regard to the permanent placement of his brother's orphaned children, made it hard to ignore what was being said.

"Prowlers? Really? I can't believe you didn't phone the police last night," Samantha told her companion.

When the other woman shook her head, her reddish-blond hair swung in a silky cascade that partially hid her cheeks from view. Although her voice was softer, Thad was able to hear her reply.

"I didn't find anything missing. It was no big deal."

One underlying sense grabbed Thad and refused

to let go. *Fear.* An unmistakable tinge of tension and dread. She might choose to claim that the event she was discussing was no big deal but her body language said otherwise.

"That doesn't mean you shouldn't report a break-in, Lindy," Samantha argued, sounding as if she were a parent lecturing a foolish child.

Thad's brow creased. *Lindy?* That name was unusual enough to ring a bell but he couldn't quite place where he'd heard it.

When the young woman lifted her chin and he could see her profile more clearly he was immediately struck by her natural beauty. And by a deepening sense that she was terribly vulnerable, although if anyone had asked him why he felt that way, he'd have been at a loss to explain.

Her voice rose. "I don't intend to make waves and take a chance on losing custody of my son again. You, of all people, should understand."

Ah, so *that* was her problem, Thad mused. He could definitely identify. He knew Samantha had only been doing her job as a volunteer for CASA, Court-Appointed Special Advocates for children, when she had recommended that his late brother's kids be adopted by outsiders, but he was still struggling to accept it.

"Everything worked out fine the last time we went to court," Samantha reminded her companion. "You can trust the police. You'll have to learn to do that, if and when you apply to become a CASA volunteer yourself, like you said you might."

"I trust you more. That's why I asked you to meet me here. I wanted you to know what happened. Just in case. You're not assigned to look out for Danny anymore so there's no conflict of interest. Right?"

"This has nothing to do with what happened in the past. I'm your friend. And I'm telling you to use your head. Make a police report. Let the pros handle it."

Thad remained silent as Lindy paid for her food, turned and started to walk away without waiting for her outspoken friend to follow.

He continued to observe her wending her way through the crowd to a nearby booth. Clearly, she had problems. Perhaps serious ones. While her personal life was none of his business, he nevertheless felt concerned. It didn't matter that such feelings made no sense. He was used to following his instincts. Doing so had kept him alive when he was overseas and it was a part of his character he nurtured.

The woman called Lindy never looked back. Never seemed to notice that she had attracted his attention.

Thad paused long enough to say a quick, silent

prayer for her before stepping up to the counter, smiling at the clerk and placing his own order.

Lindy sat back in the booth and folded her arms. She was feeling a chill in spite of her designer jeans, sweater and embroidered denim jacket. "You might as well give it a rest, Sam. I'm not changing my mind."

"Then at least let me tell John."

"Not on your life. Your husband's too good a cop. There's no way he'd keep his mouth shut, not even if you asked him to. The guys who broke in were probably just dumb kids looking for drug or booze money."

"The way you described them, they didn't sound like typical juvenile delinquents."

"They grow 'em big around here. I think it's the Ozark water," Lindy said, managing to smile past her burgeoning feelings of guilt over the deception she felt was so necessary. If she once mentioned the prowlers' specific threats, she was certain Sam would feel compelled to inform her husband—and that must not happen.

"Um. Speaking of kids, how's Danny holding up?" Samantha asked.

"He's okay."

"Good. You need to start taking him to church, you know."

"What brought that on? Are you worried that I'm not being a good enough mother?"

"Of course not. It's time Danny made some new, happy memories, that's all." Sam chuckled wryly. "You won't believe who got roped in as Sunday school teacher for the second and third grade boys' class at Serenity Chapel."

"No clue." Lindy picked up a narrow slice of steaming veggie pizza, inhaling the enticing aroma before taking a cautious bite.

"Thad Pearson. Didn't you notice him in line behind us when we ordered?"

"You mean the guy who took over Pearson Products?"

"Uh-huh. Have you met?"

"Not exactly. I saw him from a distance when I dropped off my résumé. He's certainly not the kind of person I'd picture as a Sunday school teacher."

"Me, either. But he does an amazing job with the kids. It's too bad he couldn't adopt his brother's orphans."

"Why not?" Lindy took another bite.

"PTSD. He got a medical discharge from the marines because of post-traumatic stress. Unfortunately, that meant, as a CASA representative, I couldn't recommend him as a prospective parent, even if I'd wanted to." She focused her gaze across the room and brightened, her smile becoming a broad grin. "Well, butter me up and call me a biscuit. Here he comes."

Lindy swiveled in her seat. The man was dark haired, muscular, athletic looking and wearing jeans that were worn but clean. He also had on a red polo shirt and matching jacket which bore the Pearson Products logo.

She was about to avert her gaze when it caught his and lingered a heartbeat too long. Blushing, she sank down in her seat and began wishing she could slide all the way under the table, especially when Samantha waved and hollered, "Thad! Over here."

Lindy gaped. "What did you do *that* for?"

"So I could properly introduce you to Danny's Sunday school teacher."

"I never promised I'd start going back to church."

"Ah, but you will. For Danny's sake, of course."

The hulking figure who soon hovered over Lindy made her feel as small as a child herself.

"Thad, this is Lindy Southerland," Samantha said. "She has a son the same age as your nephew, Timmy, and I was just telling her about how the kids in your class at Serenity Chapel love having you as their teacher."

"Pleased to meet you." He nodded to Lindy as he answered Samantha. "I do my best."

To Lindy's surprise, the man looked almost as ill at ease as she felt. Was he glancing around the cramped dining area because he was wishing he could make a polite getaway?

"Please, join us. We have lots of room," Samantha insisted. She checked her watch. "As a matter of fact, you can take my chair. I have to be getting back to the hospital ASAP. Nearly every bed in my wing is full. Doctors can get away with taking long lunches but we nurses don't dare." She gathered up her jacket and trash, slid out, took Thad's drink from him and placed it on the table opposite Lindy before rushing off.

For a few long seconds, Lindy wondered if the man was going to grab his soda and flee, but he didn't. Shrugging, he sat down with a resigned air, nodded another silent greeting and began to unwrap his foot-long sandwich.

"I apologize," Lindy said, feeling her cheeks burn. "Samantha sometimes gets carried away."

"No problem. As long as it's all right with you."

As soon as she said, "Sure. It's fine," he picked up his sub and began to eat.

Lindy felt strange sitting across the narrow table from a man—any man. Since being widowed she'd already had to withstand a few well-meaning efforts at matchmaking and had had no trouble doing so. Consequently, it was awkward to find herself trapped in this kind of social situation.

If the attractive man had not seemed so resigned to her presence, she might have left without finishing her lunch. Since he was essentially ignoring her, however, she had no such compunctions. She wasn't sure what PTSD entailed but she figured polite silence couldn't hurt him.

Half of Thad's food was gone before he spoke another word. "So, you have a little boy?"

"Yes. Danny."

His brow knit. He studied her. "Southerland. Any relation to the accountant who got himself shot a while back?"

Well, *that* was certainly blunt enough. Thad Pearson might be a man of few words but the ones he did use were definitely to the point. "Yes," Lindy said. Her chin jutted. "Ben was my husband. And he was an investment counselor, not an accountant."

"Sorry. I lost my only brother about a year ago."

"I know. How are his kids doing?"

"Really well, thanks." He finally smiled, sort of, giving Lindy a strange, tingling sensation and making her wish he had remained stoic. "They're great kids. Megan is so young she's adjusted the best. Tim and Paul are coming along, too. Jill and Mitch Andrews make much better parents than I thought they would. Do you know them?"

"I think I used to see them at church. Your brother and his wife, too. They were a lovely family."

Uh-oh, I said too much, Lindy decided when

she saw his smile fade. The way he was staring at her made her uncomfortable, although she could not have said *why* if her life had depended upon it. There was no anger in his expression, nor was it the kind of intense look she sometimes got from single guys. Thad didn't act as if he wanted to date her. He seemed to be trying to understand her instead.

That would be a good trick, she thought cynically. Since she didn't have a clue what made her tick, there was *no* chance a stranger would be able to figure her out.

Choosing to simply finish the final bites of her pizza, she wiped her fingers on a napkin and started to clear her side of the table.

Before she could rise, however, Thad said, "Wait," reached for her hand and laid his over it. There was no coercion, no threat and certainly no intimacy. She felt as if his touch was meant to convey empathy.

"I lost my dad when I was pretty young," he explained. "It was my older brother, Rob, and my life in the military that saved me. Literally. I'll never be able to repay that debt but I keep trying. No matter how hard you work at it, you can't be a father to Danny."

She tried to pull free her hand, although not hard enough to strain, and the intensity of his dark gaze deepened.

"Hear me out. The kid needs men in his life," Thad said gently. "Bring him to my class Sunday mornings or take him anywhere else. I don't care. Just find him somebody to look up to. For his sake."

This time, when she eased away, he let her go. She wasn't about to listen to advice from a stranger, even though they had both experienced traumatic pasts.

Lindy swept her crumpled napkin into her little pizza box, grabbed her empty soda cup and stood. She wanted to come up with some witty remark in parting but the man's words were tying her tongue. So was the realization that he was probably right.

Just last night, after the prowlers had left, Danny had said he wished his father was there so he could feel safer. No matter how hard she tried to compensate, she could not be Ben.

She didn't want to find someone else like him, either. Her late husband had been a liar and a thief and his short temper had left bruises on both her and—at the end—their son. She would never place Danny anywhere near a physically abusive relationship again. Never.

Halfway to the trash receptacle Lindy turned and glanced back. Thad was sitting very still, watching her, yet there was no judgment in his expression. On the contrary, it was so benevolent it made her feel as if she were wrapped in a warm, cozy blanket that would invisibly protect her from the world's wickedness.

"I'll think about it," Lindy said quietly and saw him begin to nod before she looked away.

Somewhere in the depths of her confusion about practically everything in life, she sensed that she had already made that decision. Danny could benefit from knowing Thad Pearson. Therefore, she would take him to Sunday school. It might even be easier to convince herself to leave him in the care of *that* teacher than any of the ones at his elementary school.

Lindy smiled. There was an additional benefit for a mother who could hardly bear to let her only child out of her sight. At church, she could linger in the hallway outside Danny's classroom and no one would think it a bit odd.

No one except, perhaps, his understanding teacher.

TWO

There weren't many conundrums that bothered Thad Pearson for very long. After the years he'd spent in war zones, he was used to meeting challenges head-on. Right now, he figured he must be thinking about battle casualties again due to the familiar, wounded aura around the woman Samantha had railroaded him into eating with.

Lindy Southerland's personal problems were probably common knowledge in Serenity, Arkansas, and for once he wished he'd paid more attention to gossip. He knew she was a widow because her husband had died a violent death in some kind of gang shoot-out, but that was about all.

"It's enough," Thad murmured, dumping his trash and heading for the café door. He didn't have to know a lot about the kids he worked with to help them. Besides, that woman might never drum up enough courage to actually bring Danny to his class.

Mrs. Southerland was clearly scared to death.

Not having known her prior to returning to the States, he had no idea if her unsettled persona was a new development or if she'd always been the nervous type. Either way, living with someone like that couldn't be easy on the boy. If Danny was about the same age as his nephew, Timmy, then he was seven or eight. Not too young to understand simple logic or too old to be reached via kindness. A good age.

Thad checked his watch. He'd promised to refill the break room fridge with sodas for his crew and figured this was as good a time as any to swing by the store. He'd been trying to loosen up and not run the Pearson kitchen-gadget business with his usual military precision, but he knew he was still a long way from being the hassle-free kind of boss his brother, Rob, had been. Providing free sodas would be another step in the right direction.

Pushing his cart to the nearest of the two checkout stands at the little local market, he was surprised to recognize a familiar voice coming from the customer ahead of him in line.

"But it *has* to be good," Lindy Southerland was insisting to the clerk. "I put plenty of money in that account a few days ago."

When she exchanged that debit card for a credit card with a shake of her head, Thad was struck by how beautiful her reddish-blond hair was when it swung. During lunch he'd noticed it was long and framed her heart-shaped face but he'd been look-ing so intently into her green eyes, trying to read her thoughts, he hadn't paid attention to much else. Now, however, he could appreciate the graceful way her hands were moving as she held them out, palms up, in supplication.

Lindy's next words fit the pose perfectly. "What? That's impossible. I almost never use that card. It can't be maxed out."

"It isn't," the clerk said. "It's been canceled."

"No way."

Thad saw Lindy's confusion and realized she was too frustrated to be thinking clearly. He stepped forward and opened his wallet. "Here. Let me get this for you."

The emerald eyes widened when they met his. Recognition dawned. "No, thank you. I can take care of it." She was rummaging in her copious shoulder bag. "I don't usually carry my checkbook but it may be in here."

"Well, since we're holding up the line, how about I bail you out temporarily? You can pay me back after you figure out what's wrong with your cards."

Lindy sighed noisily. "I guess that will be okay. We are both friends of Samantha."

Thad didn't think this was the right time to in-form her that he was less a friend of Samantha Rochard, now Waltham, than he was a former adversary. Oh, they had made their peace regarding the permanent placement of his niece and two nephews but that didn't make them buddies. Thad could count his close friends on the fingers of one hand without using half the digits. His military doctors had been right when they'd warned him that he might not relate well to most folks, although he was beginning to warm up to Jill and Mitch, probably because of their connection to his brother's children.

Paying his own bill as well as Lindy's, Thad carried their groceries while she walked beside him and continued to paw through her purse.

"Which car is yours?" he asked.

"What? Oh, the silver one over there."

"Nice."

"It was my husband's," she said flatly. "It's paid for and it gets good gas mileage so I kept it. I suppose I should have traded it in on a smaller model but I just never got around to it."

"There's nothing wrong with a luxury car. Where do you want this stuff? In the trunk?"

"Yes." She pressed a button on her key ring and the trunk unlatched with a click. "Thanks. I'll pay you back as soon as I get everything sorted out."

"No hurry. You know where to find me on Sunday mornings. I'm looking forward to meeting Danny." The startled expression on her face made him chuckle wryly. "Not very subtle, am I?"

"No. Not very." She began to smile and reached out, clearly offering to shake his hand.

Thad shifted his own grocery bags so he could oblige. He hadn't anticipated feeling her tremble. It was not that cold for a short walk outside.

Rather than release her immediately, he held on long enough to ask, "What is it? What else is wrong?"

"Nothing, I..."

"Don't you know it's a sin to lie to a Sunday school teacher?"

"It's a sin to lie to anybody," Lindy said. She seemed to be struggling with a decision for a few moments before she sighed and spoke again. "It's a long story. My house was burglarized recently. I surprised them in the act so I didn't think anything was stolen." Her forehead furrowed. "Now, I'm not sure. I mean, the cards are still in my purse. They can't have been used."

So *that* was the rest of the story he'd partially overheard. "You don't have to have a card in hand to debit to it, you know. Look at sales on the internet. All you have to do is type in the right numbers and it's a done deal."

She paled and swayed slightly. "Oh, dear."

"What did the police say about your break-in?" Thad asked, knowing what she'd probably say.

"I didn't call them."

"You should have." He scowled, hoping his

opinion would make her change her mind. "What stopped you?"

"It's complicated."

"Okay. Look, I have a little experience with computers. If you'll let me, I'd like to help you."

"What can you possibly do?"

"Start by checking your accounts to see when they were tampered with, file a claim to have the money returned, then tighten up security to make sure nobody can do any more damage." He paused, smiling at the irrationality of his suggestions and wondering why he'd made them. "Or, you could just swing by the bank on your way home and do all that in person."

Lindy began to shake her head. "I can't. My husband insisted we keep our accounts in Atlanta, even after we moved here, and I never got around to changing to a local bank."

"Then my offer stands. I learned a lot of useful tricks while I was working for Uncle Sam. I'm pretty sure I can help you."

"I'd heard you were a soldier. I had no idea that job involved computers."

"We had guns, too," Thad said, continuing to smile for her benefit. "I was taught to handle both." He eyed an old blue pickup that was parked several spaces away. "There's my truck. Since you didn't buy any perishables you can follow me to my office and we can get started right away."

"I don't know, I…"

He held up his free hand as though taking an oath. "I promise you. I am one of the good guys. I even have the medals to prove it. I can dig them out and show you if necessary."

"I'll take your word for it."

"Good, then hop in your car and let's go."

"Why are you doing this?" Lindy asked, still acting hesitant.

"Because you look like somebody who needs help and I'm in a position to offer it, that's all. No ulterior motives. Scout's honor."

It was easy to tell she remained anxious. He assumed that was because of those useless bank cards and the fact that someone had violated her privacy. He could understand feeling that way. He just hoped she would take him up on his offer instead of changing her mind and driving off.

Watching in his rearview mirror, he was relieved to see the silver sedan pull out and fall smoothly into line behind him. She was going to let him help. Good. If he'd ever met someone who needed a friend it was Lindy Southerland.

Why care? he asked himself. That was an excellent question. Perhaps it was because of the woman's demeanor. Or maybe it was meeting a widow who was raising her child alone that had tapped into his conscience and created such a strong desire to offer assistance.

He'd seen plenty of widows overseas; enough to last him a lifetime. And every time his work had fractured more families, his gut had tied in bigger knots. Knots that still lingered and had resulted in a medical discharge in spite of his continued desire to serve.

The doctors who had judged him no longer fit for duty hadn't understood. Nobody did. There was no job Thad had ever tackled that he hadn't approached with complete dedication. That was why he'd assumed personal responsibility for the outcome of every skirmish and why the shrinks who had debriefed him had insisted he be sent back to civilian life.

Well, here he was. And, in retrospect, his presence had been advantageous after Rob and Ellen had died in the fire that Ellen's sister, Natalie, had caused. But that didn't make life fair; not for his lost brother, not for Rob's orphaned kids who had been given to people who were not even kin, not for all the survivors who had to carry on in spite of broken hearts.

That needless sense of loss continued to disturb Thad but not in the same way it had at first. His personal faith had faltered initially, then had deepened in the aftermath of the tragedy, yet he was still searching for a satisfactory explanation for all the pain his family had suffered.

Perhaps he always would.

* * *

Lindy knew she was being foolish to trust a virtual stranger but there had been something about Thad Pearson that had emotionally connected him to her. From the moment he had touched her hand and shown such concern for Danny, she had liked him. She couldn't help herself.

But do I dare trust him this much? she asked silently. If she'd been the least bit computer savvy or had known someone else who might be willing to go to bat for her, she wouldn't have turned to Thad. However, since he was not only handy but had dropped into her life at exactly the right time, as if heaven-sent, she felt compelled to let him try to help. Worst case scenario, she'd have to change the passwords on a few accounts. Other than that, she couldn't see any big risk.

Sensing movement out of the corner of her eye, Lindy glanced into her side mirror. Speaking of risks, what did the driver of that big, white, dual-cab pickup think he was doing? This narrow section of road was no place to try to squeeze by.

Her hands tightened on the wheel. The other truck had pulled even with her and was easing to the right, encroaching on her lane.

She tapped the brakes, slowing to give the larger vehicle room to drop in between her and Thad. Since she knew where they were headed, she didn't need to stay right on his bumper. Besides, somebody had to do something before that other driver caused a wreck.

Lindy fell back, waiting for the more massive truck to sail on by. It did exactly the opposite, pacing her exactly.

Scowling, she glanced over, trying to see who was driving, but was thwarted because the truck sat so much higher off the ground than her car. Its broad side door and right fender stayed even with her no matter how she varied her speed.

Her heart pounded. Her breathing grew shallow, rapid. Had Thad noticed what was going on? It sure didn't look like it.

Again, Lindy changed speed, shoving the gas pedal to the floor. Forty became fifty. Then fifty-five.

The rear of Thad's truck loomed ahead. She thought she saw his head turn, saw him look back.

Suddenly, the white truck swerved.

Slammed into the side of her sedan.

Hit hard enough to shove her onto the narrow shoulder!

Metal crunched and grated. Gravel flew. She almost overcorrected and went into a ditch, then regained the edge of the roadway and came to a stop as the reckless driver accelerated and sped away.

Incredulous, she just sat there, her fingers clamped to the steering wheel, her eyes wide. Staring blankly.

The driver who had forced her off the road passed Thad as if his truck were standing still and disappeared around a curve.

She could barely breathe, barely think straight.

This was turning into the second worst day of her life.

Thad stopped the moment he realized what had happened. Jumping from his truck he ran back to Lindy. "Are you all right?"

The side window rolled smoothly down. Her breath was condensing into visible clouds and her complexion had lost its rosy glow. "Did you see that? That idiot was trying to *wreck* me!"

"Sure looked that way." Thad continued to check the road as he spoke in case the heavy-duty truck came back. "I thought he just wanted to pass us until I saw him deliberately ram you." He was leaning against her car with both hands capping the edge of the door over the window slot. "Who was he?"

"I don't have the slightest idea. I didn't recognize his truck, either." She peered forward and winced. "How bad is the damage?"

"Looks mostly cosmetic," Thad said. "Though you should still have a garage check over the car before we go on."

Lindy let go of the steering wheel and stared

at her hands, watching them shake. "I'm not sure I'm ready to drive again, anyway."

"No problem." Straightening, Thad slipped his cell phone from the clip on his belt, flipped it open and stepped away from her car to speak. He didn't ask Lindy's permission. He simply called the sheriff.

She was tugging at his elbow long before he finished the call but he persisted. "That's right. Hit-and-run. Highway 9, south of town. Nobody's injured. A guy in a white truck sideswiped Mrs. Southerland's car then took off. No. We didn't get a license number and we didn't know the driver."

Lindy yanked on his arm. "Stop!"

He ignored her. "It's pretty cold for us to wait out here. How about we leave the car as it sits and I take her with me to the warehouse? Is that all right with you?" He recited the license plate number and make of her vehicle. "Okay. If you have any questions for us, you can reach us at this number. It's my cell. Or at Pearson Products. We're headed there." He ended the call with, "Right. Thanks."

"What did you do *that* for?"

Lindy was practically screeching at him so he reached to place a calming hand on her shoulder. To his amazement, she ducked as if expecting a blow.

Thad raised both hands and backed away.

"Whoa. I'm not going to hurt you. Just calm down. You've had quite a shock."

"I *told* you I didn't want the authorities involved in my business. Why did you have to call them?"

"Oh, I don't know. Maybe because somebody almost rolled your car into a ball—with you in it." He knew he'd spoken gruffly but he didn't know how else he was going to get through to this stubborn, irrational woman.

Lindy covered her face with her hands.

Thad started to reach for her, then stopped himself. She'd already indicated reluctance to accept physical comforting. He could get himself into deep trouble by trying to give it again.

Instead, he waited patiently until she pulled herself together, then nodded toward his pickup. "My ride's not fancy, but right now that's our only transportation. Unless you want to wait out here for the cops and freeze to death, I suggest you come with me the way I told them you would."

She stood so still for a few moments he wondered if she was going to refuse. Finally, she seemed to regain her composure. "I'll need my purse. And I suppose I should take the groceries in case they tow my car."

"I'm assuming they will," Thad said. It was a relief to see her acting more stable. "They probably won't need your keys so you'd better pull them. The dispatcher said they were really busy today.

Since nobody was hurt here, it may take them a while to respond and we don't want your car stolen before they arrive."

Lindy almost laughed. At least Thad thought she did. She'd been so upset before, it was hard to tell how she was feeling until he heard the sarcasm in her tone when she said, "The way my life's been going lately, I wouldn't be a bit surprised. I'd expect it."

He stood back while she unlocked the trunk, then carried her purchases to his truck and placed the plastic bags in the cab between the driver and passenger seats. The way he saw it, he was already on thin ice with this woman and having a pile of groceries as a buffer between them was to his advantage.

Did he wish he hadn't volunteered to help her? Not really. If he hadn't been there when she'd almost wrecked, she'd have been stranded, particularly because she was so against police involvement.

Thad observed her as he held open the passenger door and she climbed in. She seemed pretty normal in most ways, so why was she so scared of the cops? Could there be a connection between her current problems and her late husband's criminal activities? Had she been personally involved?

No. No way, his instincts insisted. He'd know if Lindy was a crook at heart. Truth to tell, she seemed so totally innocent it was laughable. He could far more easily imagine her as a helpless lamb being circled by a pack of hungry wolves than the other way around.

That picture of helplessness stuck in his mind as he rounded the truck and slid behind the wheel. If he were to consider the accident he had just witnessed as a deliberate attack, how might that change his tactics going forward?

He cast a sidelong glance at the woman riding beside him. She was obviously still tense. Her hands were clasped around the strap of her purse and she was holding on to it as if she were suspended above a bottomless chasm by that one, thin strip of leather.

Strange notions kept surfacing, insisting to Thad that he had been put there to provide an anchor for Lindy's lifeline. Was that possible? Sure. Why not? If someone had asked him a few years ago what he'd be doing these days, he would never have guessed he'd be managing a kitchen-gadget business in a little Ozark town. And if they'd suggested he'd be playing bodyguard to a pretty but unstable widow, too, he'd have laughed in their faces.

So, what now? Only one thing was certain. No matter what his original motives had been or how circumstances had conspired to draw him into this woman's problems, he was committed. He knew Lindy Southerland needed help and it was his duty to provide it. Period.

THREE

Pearson Products was located next to the single-runway Serenity airport outside town. Lindy had passed the site often but other than the one time she had tried to apply for a job there, she'd never had reason to stop.

As Thad drove around to the rear of the largest metal building, she was struck by how isolated the manufacturing and shipping complex seemed. The hardwood trees on the surrounding hills were bare but would soon begin to bud, and by summer the open area would feel like a tiny island amid a sea of green leaves.

If there had not been other cars parked there, she might have been more uneasy. "I never realized how far out of town this place is. It's really secluded."

"It wasn't always." Thad pointed. "Rob and Ellen used to have a house attached to their office on the far end of this long building. You can still see the foundation. I made my office in the warehouse instead of rebuilding after the fire."

"So, you don't live out here like they did?"

"No. I have a little place off Old Sturkie Road. It isn't fancy. I don't spend a lot of time there."

She chose to open her own door rather than wait for Thad to do it. Ben had always made a big deal of holding doors for her and otherwise treating her gallantly in public, though he'd abused her in private, so Lindy now insisted on fending for herself. It wasn't that she objected to a man showing good manners, it simply seemed intrinsically necessary for her to demonstrate self-reliance as often as possible.

If Thad minded her behaving so independently he didn't give any sign of it. Smiling, he directed her to the rear entrance to the warehouse and caught the heavyweight metal door behind her as she passed through. The area was open and airy like a barn, yet bore the chemical odor of new plastic. It wasn't an unpleasant smell but it was a noticeable change from the crispness of the February air outdoors.

"This is our shipping department," Thad said, pointing to rows of bins and shelves filled with brightly colored kitchen tools and several long tables. "You probably know most of these folks better than I do. That's Margaret over there in the brown sweater doing the packing and Louise

Williams pulling orders. Vernon Betts looks after the factory and Angela runs the mail room."

Lindy raised a hand to wave when Louise looked up and smiled. "I do recognize a few faces. We moved to Serenity a couple years ago but I really haven't gotten out much."

"I know what you mean. I've been so tied up in trying to salvage this business I don't have time to socialize, either. If it wasn't for church, I'd probably be a hermit."

She followed Thad as he led the way to a rudimentary office located at one end of the cavernous, rectangular building. That area was anything but posh. The floor was concrete, the walls unpainted plasterboard. There were bundles of assorted cardboard boxes stacked in one corner. The massive, oak desk was so messy it looked as if someone had upended a carton of trash in the middle of it, then stirred the pile of paper with the blade of a shovel.

Lindy had to smile. "I love your filing system. How's that working out for you?"

"Poorly." One corner of his mouth quirked and his dark eyes sparkled. "I know I need help. I just don't want to hire and then have to lay off somebody. Orders are sporadic since Rob died and I can never be sure how the cash flow will hold up. Ellen used to process orders while her sister, Natalie, kept the books." He grimaced. "You probably heard how that turned out."

"The embezzlement? Yes. I'm sorry." Lindy's fingers itched to get a chance to sort through the messy piles of paperwork.

"Tell you what," she said, eyeing his desktop. "While you try to figure out what happened to my credit, why don't I start sorting this stuff into some semblance of order?"

"I don't know..."

"Well, I do," she said flatly. "You're helping me and I'm going to return the favor." She pushed up the left sleeve of her jacket to check her watch. "I can stay until just before three when I have to pick up Danny at school."

Thad nodded. "It's a deal. Let me know when it's time and I'll run you back into town."

"If you do that, I'll owe you even more hours of work here," Lindy said.

She was delighted to see him grin and hear him say, "Uh-huh. That's kind of what I'd figured."

Thad was so engrossed in his computer search he let Lindy answer the business phone. He had to smile at how professional her "Pearson Products. How may I help you?" sounded. It was good to have an accomplished executive assistant, if only for one afternoon.

She made a face as she covered the mouthpiece and held out the receiver. "It's the sheriff. They've taken my car into town and parked it behind the station. We can pick it up any time."

"Okay. Tell them I'm going to call Seth Whitfield at the garage and have him check it over first. You shouldn't drive it until we know it's safe." To his surprise, Lindy looked anything but pleased.

She put the phone back to her ear. "Thank you, Sheriff. Mr. Pearson has suggested that I have the car examined by a mechanic but I'll take your word for it that it's roadworthy. We'll be there before three."

As soon as she'd hung up he questioned her. "What was *that?*"

"That was me, taking care of myself and making my own decisions," Lindy said firmly. "I decided to skip the expense of taking the car to a repairman. The sheriff assures me the damage is only cosmetic."

"Okay. I can see you don't want car advice." He swiveled in his chair and gestured toward the computer screen. "However, I think you should look at what I've found online."

"What?"

Thad allowed her to look over his shoulder while he brought up screen after screen. Then, he ended with her official credit rating and heard her gasp.

"I didn't know they went that low," she moaned.

"Neither did I until I saw yours. What's going

on? This shows that you maxed out your credit cards and failed to pay the minimum so they were all canceled."

"No!" It was nearly a shout. "I don't use any credit cards unless I absolutely have to. What about my debit card? Did you check that?"

"I'll need your account number and password," Thad said. He started to get up so she could take his place at the keyboard.

Instead, she merely recited a short sequence of numbers. He typed them in. He could sense Lindy's closeness behind him and hear her rapid breathing. The woman was clearly agitated. He didn't blame her.

The checking account balance blinked onto the screen, accompanied by Lindy's sharp intake of breath. "That's impossible. I just transferred money into that account from my savings." She leaned closer. "Can you check that, too?"

"Sure." He paged down and clicked on the listing.

Lindy's squeal of astonishment was so loud and unexpected it made him jump. He felt her hand rest on his shoulder only long enough for her to say, "Sorry."

"I take it you didn't know you were broke."

"I'm *not*." She left him and slumped into the only other chair in the room after clearing it of bundles of product brochures. "I have money. At least I did. The investment company my husband worked for has been depositing a portion of his unused sick leave in my account every month and there was a life insurance settlement, too. I paid off my mortgage with that so I wouldn't have a lot of big expenses."

Thad leaned back and turned his desk chair to face her. "Okay. Suppose I believe you…"

"What do you mean, *suppose?* It's the truth."

"Poor choice of words. Sorry. What I should have said is, given your belief that you had sufficient funds in your accounts and plenty of room to charge more purchases on your credit and debit cards, what do you think happened to all the money?"

"How should *I* know?"

He watched her get to her feet and begin to pace what little space the office afforded. He had assumed that he could solve her problems with a few swift keystrokes after he located a simple glitch. This was far more complicated than that. If he believed her—and he did—then she had been hacked. Big time.

"Who would want to falsify records and ruin you?" Thad asked.

When Lindy whirled and gawked at him, he was certain he'd asked the right question. "What do you mean?"

"Just what I said. This is no computer mix-up.

It's deliberate. Somebody wants you broke and they've just about succeeded in making that happen. What I need to know is, why? Who's that mad at you, Lindy?"

"Nobody." She returned to the chair and perched on its edge, leaning her elbows on her knees and cupping her face in her hands.

"Okay," he drawled, choosing his words carefully, "then who might still have it in for your late husband?"

Her head snapped up. Her jaw dropped. It took several long seconds for her to regain her composure and in that short space of time, Thad saw myriad conflicting emotions. The final one looked a lot like resignation.

"You don't have to tell me a thing," Thad said. "But you should confide in someone, preferably somebody in law enforcement. You do see that, don't you?"

Standing again, she pulled her jacket tighter, folded her arms across her chest and shook her head. "No. Absolutely not."

"What are you afraid of?"

"Who says I'm afraid?"

"You do. It's written all over you. And there's no reason to feel that way when you have an alternative. Talk to the police. Let them help you."

"I have nothing to say to them. I'll phone the bank in Atlanta and the other credit card companies, explain the problem, and everything will be fine. You said so yourself."

"That was before I saw the records." Thad stood but didn't try to approach her. He could tell how close she was to the breaking point and didn't want to do anything that might push her too far. Nevertheless, he felt obliged to try to convince her to be sensible.

He found an empty place for his hip on the edge of the desk and struck a nonchalant pose by perching there. "Look, lady, you're in big trouble. Somebody has hacked into your accounts and left you destitute. Unless you're carrying a wad of cash in your purse, you can't even buy yourself a hamburger right now. Understand?"

"Unfortunately, yes."

"The way I see it, you have two choices. You can either report the theft and let the proper authorities step in or you can give up and let the bad guys walk off with your money—not to mention whatever they might also try to charge against your credit in the future."

He could tell by the way her eyes misted that he had her full attention so he plunged ahead. "Give me one good reason why I shouldn't call the cops for you."

Lindy's mouth opened. No words came. Thad didn't need to hear any. The unbridled fear emanating from her reached him all the way across the office and raised the hair on the nape of his neck.

"They threatened you," he said flatly. "I should have known. What did they say?"

Lindy pressed her lips tightly together, shook her head and averted her gaze.

Thad decided to take the chance of approaching, of gently grasping her shoulders so she'd have no choice but to look at him. When she didn't jump at his touch or try to slap his face the way he was afraid she might, he took it as a positive sign.

"Look, if you keep their threats to yourself, they win," Thad said. "Think about it. The only control they have over you is by intimidation. I know you're a strong woman. You'd have to be to have weathered the trials I've heard about." He paused, intending to censor his next statement, then let it continue unedited. "I'm going to help you whether you like it or not. I feel as if we were meant to meet so I could. Does that make sense?"

"No." Lindy's tone was weak, her voice tremulous.

Releasing her and distancing himself, Thad smiled. "It doesn't to me, either, but that's how I feel."

"You don't want to get mixed up in my troubles."

"It's already too late. I promised God a long

time ago that if He'd let me live, I'd do all I could to help the helpless for the rest of my life."

He immediately raised his hands, palms out, as if surrendering. "Don't get mad. I'm not calling you helpless. I'm just telling you the story the way it happened. My unit was pinned down by sniper fire and I'd taken a bullet in the shoulder. I figure, since I'm standing here having this conversation with you, I need to remember that promise. That's all."

"A bullet in the shoulder?" Lindy sighed deeply and released the breath with a visible shudder. "We've got more in common than I thought."

Thad didn't realize what she'd meant until she took off her jacket, pushed up the softer sleeve of the sweater beneath and revealed a scar that cut a shallow groove across her upper arm.

Thad had seen lots of worse injuries, yet his gut knotted. Someone had hurt this sweet, innocent woman in the past and those same people might now be planning to do her further harm. He was going to see that they—or anyone else—didn't get away with it.

"What happened?" His voice was gentle even though his fists were clenched.

"The shot that passed through my husband grazed my arm. We were both protecting Danny. Ben died trying to keep us safe."

"I'm so sorry. I had no idea."

"Most people don't know the whole story. They're happy to blame Ben for everything and say he deserved whatever he got. It's a lot more complicated than that."

"The men who killed your husband—are they still after you?"

Lindy slowly shook her head. "They can't be. Two died in the same gunfight and a third was arrested later. The problem is, I didn't know for sure whether or not there were others who might have it in for us—until last night."

"Are you positive the men who messed with your credit are from the same gang?"

"No. But I can't afford to take the chance that they were lying when they threatened me. They mentioned Ben. That was enough."

"And I suppose they also told you to avoid the police?"

"Yes. They said they'd be back and hurt Danny and me if I reported the break-in. What could I do? I have no way to fight them. I don't even know who they are."

Deep in thought, Thad scowled. "Why pick on you? And why now, after so much time has passed? What could they want? Was there a lot of cash in your accounts?"

"A couple thousand, and maybe another four if

you add up all the unused credit I thought I had on the cards. It still isn't much, even with what they managed to steal in cash advances."

"Right. It doesn't make sense to go to that trouble."

Lindy huffed. "Well, at least we agree on something."

"I have an idea."

"If it has anything to do with calling the police, forget it."

"Actually, no," Thad said. "I still maintain that you're making a big mistake but I think I see a way for you to get by while we figure this out."

"We, Kemosabe?"

He was glad to see her starting to smile. His own grin spread as the plan came together in his mind. "See, that's your problem. You're going about this like a lone ranger when you need friends. How would you like a job?"

"You can't afford me."

"I can't guarantee long-term employment, but as you can see, I have a desperate need for someone who can organize this office." His arm passed over the clutter she had barely had time to touch, let alone sort properly. "First, we'll set up a new bank account for you and tell whoever has been sending monthly checks to deposit them locally instead of in Atlanta."

Hope shone in her eyes and her smile broadened.

"It's not the perfect solution but it will allow you to live fairly normally until something else happens."

The grin waned. "Like what?"

"I don't know. I don't want you to have any more trouble but if they do try anything else, we'll be waiting. Sign up for online banking and I can imbed an automatic notification trigger in your new accounts so we'll know the second someone else tries to access them. Maybe that way they'll tip us off."

"Okay, then what?"

He was going to say that then they could contact the police but kept that to himself. *One day at a time,* Thad thought. One day, one problem, one solution at a time. Arranged properly, those sensible steps could lead to the answers Lindy needed.

And if they didn't? If they didn't, he'd simply keep her employed and figure out a way to pay her, even if her wages had to come out of his own pocket.

That notion made him smile. Since his new executive assistant was about to start handling the company books, he hoped it wouldn't come to that. He was positive she'd pitch a royal fit if she learned she was being subsidized.

Sobering, Thad admitted to himself that wages were the least of his worries. Unless he could figure out how to guard Lindy and her son when they were at home, no amount of money was going to be enough to keep her from further harm.

The way he saw it, the first thing he had to do was convince her to *let* him guard them.

He chuckled softly. It would probably be easier to hire a backhoe to dig a moat around her house and fill it with hungry alligators than it would be to talk her into letting anybody look after her the way he wanted to.

FOUR

Lindy picked up her car, parted from Thad and drove directly to the school where she waited on the sidewalk outside Danny's classroom. The bell rang and a hoard of laughing, chattering children dashed past. The moment her son spotted her, he grinned from ear to ear.

"Hi. Guess what? I got an A on my spelling test!"

"That's wonderful, honey." She relieved him of his heavy backpack and escorted him toward the parking lot. Her aim was to keep him safe without scaring him. Too bad she had no idea how to accomplish that goal.

"Whoa!" Danny skidded to a stop and pointed. "What happened to the car, Mom?"

"I had a little fender bender."

"Looks like a fender smasher."

Lindy ruffled his reddish hair and grinned. "It's not as bad as it looks. And I have some good news. I found a job."

The child's eyes widened and he stared up at her. "Will I have to ride the school bus?"

"No. Nothing will change for you. My boss says I can leave work to pick you up just like I did today. As a matter of fact, I'm going to take you back to the office with me so you can meet him."

Danny stood very still and stared at the toes of his sneakers as if they were suddenly the most interesting thing he'd ever seen. "I don't wanna."

"Well, you have to. You'll be staying with me every afternoon and there's no way you can avoid meeting Mr. Pearson. Besides, he's a nice man. You'll like him."

"Uh-uh."

Rather than continue to argue, Lindy shepherded her son the rest of the way to the car, made sure he was belted in safely and got behind the wheel. There were times when she saw the boy as an adult in a child's body and other times, like now, when he looked and acted even younger than his seven-plus years. She supposed that was to be expected. Eldest and single children tended to be ultra-responsible while kids who had been traumatized sometimes regressed. With her son, elements of both influences seesawed back and forth. Right now, he was behaving like a toddler.

Danny never said a word during their drive, not even when Lindy pulled into the Pearson Products gravel lot and stopped the car.

"I made sure there was a healthy snack waiting for you inside," she said as she helped him out and hefted his pack. "I stopped at the market this morning and bought some of your favorites."

Still, he didn't answer. Lindy was thankful he at least let her take his hand and lead him into the building without throwing a tantrum. There had been times in the not-too-distant past when he'd balked at merely leaving his bedroom at home, let alone the house. Starting back to school had been a big step. Going to church again would be, too. And if Danny already knew his teacher, that would hopefully be an even easier transition.

Work momentarily ceased as they made their entrance. Lindy merely waved at the women packing merchandise and hurried Danny through the warehouse to the office.

The child had always acted withdrawn around his father but with other people he knew, he had been fairly outgoing. Until the shooting. After that he had seemed unable to relax unless they were totally alone. Maybe, once he got used to keeping her company in the office, he'd be able to loosen up and be more like his old self again.

Thad started to rise when she and Danny entered, then eased back down into his chair when Lindy silently signaled him to keep his distance.

What amazed her the most was how quickly he understood what she wanted. Not only did he tip back the chair, he laced his fingers behind his head and struck a nonchalant pose that would have fooled her if she hadn't noticed the clear concern in his eyes.

"This is Danny," Lindy said. "Danny, I want you to meet Mr. Pearson."

Instead of offering to shake hands with the boy, Thad just smiled. "Hi."

Although Danny didn't reply, Lindy did see him dart a glance toward the man. So far, so good. At least he hadn't broken away and raced out the door.

Gazing around for a place to make Danny comfortable, Lindy belatedly realized there were no empty surfaces on which he could do homework, nor was there a suitable chair for him.

She sighed and addressed her son. "Hmm. I wonder where we should put you?"

"Home," he said softly.

At that, Thad chuckled and slowly got to his feet. "Tell you what, kid," he drawled. "How would you like a room all your own, like a fort? I used to build those all the time when I was your age."

Although the child edged closer to his mother and kept her between himself and the man, he seemed interested.

Thad crossed the small room and began assembling and taping empty cardboard boxes into the square shapes used for shipping. Lindy could tell he was choosing the largest ones and quickly saw that he was making the adult equivalent of children's building blocks.

When he'd completed about fifteen he motioned to Danny. "Think this is enough? I figured we'd stack them over here, like this."

The timid boy released his mother's hand, much to her surprise, and took several steps forward. He pointed.

"Where?" Thad asked. "Here? Maybe over there? I don't quite understand."

Danny took three more steps, paused, then pointed again.

"Sorry, kid. Guess I'm dense. Where did you want these?"

"Over there, like this," Danny replied, making the final journey and grabbing the closest cardboard cube. The box was large but lightweight because it was empty. He swung it into place against the wall, then added another on top of it.

"Oh, I get it," Thad said, maintaining a serious yet friendly demeanor. "That's smart. If we stack them in the corner we won't need as many."

"Yeah," Danny replied, loud enough for his mother to hear.

Lindy was flabbergasted. Here was a child who exhibited unnatural fear of strangers, particularly big, strong men, yet he was pitching in to build a cardboard fort with Thad as if they were old friends. Amazing!

While she watched, Lindy saw her son allow Thad closer and closer, and her fondest hope was that this temporary truce would become permanent.

"Not like that," Danny said. "Put the big ones on the bottom and the little ones on top. See? They won't fall over if you do that."

"Gotcha. You're pretty smart, aren't you? How old are you? About twelve?"

The boy grinned. "Naw. I'm almost eight. But I'm big for my age."

"You sure are." Thad straightened and backed away, hands fisted on his hips. "Think that will do or should we go find more boxes and make higher walls?"

"That's good like it is," Danny said, considering their construction as if he were the architect of a skyscraper. "It needs a door."

"Hard to do without a frame," Thad said. "How about we give that some thought while you get used to your new office?"

The child giggled and looked to Lindy. "Okay, Mom?"

"Perfect. Have you thanked Mr. Pearson?"

Thad raised his hands in the air and backed away. "No need for that. We both worked on it. Now, what about furniture? Danny can't do his homework without a table and chair."

"Really, I…" Lindy's objection was cut short

by Thad's warning glance. "Right," she continued brightly. "How are you two geniuses going to make those?"

She saw her usually reticent son look up to the ex-marine as if he held the answers to all life's questions.

Thad began to grin. "I have an idea. We're pretty much out of boxes in here. Follow me."

He never looked back as he strode past Lindy to the door. It was as if he knew Danny would follow. As if he was willing him to trust. And so he did.

She stood at the office door and watched an amazing transformation occurring. Not only was Danny keeping up with Thad, he had double-timed enough to walk beside him. The sight of her timid son joining such a sizeable man in any endeavor left her speechless.

Maybe this job was more than the answer to her prayers for employment. Maybe it was for Danny's benefit, as well.

She began to smile in spite of deep concerns over her fragile financial situation. Yes, she was still very worried about the canceled credit cards and her missing money, but there were more important things in life than that. Danny's recovery and future happiness meant more to her than all the money in the world.

Even if the cause of the cyber attack on her finances was never found, the unexpected side

effects of that hacking were something to be cele-
brated. There she was, in a job she wouldn't have
gotten if she hadn't been in trouble, watching her
son warm up to a man he might never have gotten close to otherwise. How could she complain?
This was almost too good to be true.

Thad hadn't been sure his ploy would work until
he'd seen the sparkle in Danny's eyes. It was obvious that the boy's mother loved him dearly but,
somewhere along the line she'd lost her sense of
playfulness. That was where Thad had the advantage and he intended to make the most of it.

Gathering stacks of slim cartons that were still
in bundles from their delivery, he wound a short
stack in plastic wrap and handed it to Danny.
"Here you go. You carry the desktop and I'll bring
the sides."

The child was beaming when he returned to
where his mother waited. Thad was pretty happy
himself, especially considering the beatific smile
on Lindy's face when she gazed at her son.

It must be comforting to please someone that
much, he mused, refusing to let himself dwell on
that thought. It was his job to help this fractured
family and that was exactly what he was going to
do. Period. He wasn't about to picture himself as
part of it.

It had taken him months to accept the fact that

the military shrinks had been right about his mental state. Because of nightmares and flashbacks caused by the PTSD, he wasn't the right person to parent his brother's kids and it wasn't fair to make them wait for a new home until he was well again—if he ever would be.

But he did have a way with children. He might not be suited for permanent fatherhood, but he could be a true friend, a buddy, on a level that youngsters understood. That was what he was doing when he led the Sunday school class and he was determined that the same would be true of his interaction with Danny Southerland.

Placing two medium-size boxes eighteen inches apart, Thad stood back and let the boy lay the planklike package across them to serve as a table-top.

"Okay, now we need a chair."

"I can do that by myself," Danny insisted.

Watching him choose, Thad started to grin. He figured it was better to let the boy learn by making his own mistakes.

The minute Danny plunked down on the empty cardboard box he had selected as a stool, it collapsed and he fell on his back pockets, giggling.

"I think it might be better to use one with stuff in it," Thad said, joining in the laughter. "I have just the thing. You don't mind sitting on colanders, do you?"

Danny sobered. "What's that?"

"A strainer, like I use when we make spaghetti," Lindy volunteered. "They'll be in boxes. You won't even know."

Thad's grin widened when the child looked to him as if waiting for the final decision before saying, "Okay," and swiveling to concentrate on his mother. "We can make that tonight for supper, huh?"

"If you want," she said easily.

"And Mr. Pearson can come eat with us."

Thad would have laughed aloud if there hadn't been such a stricken expression on Lindy's face. He thought about relieving her anxiety by refusing the childish invitation, then decided it would be advantageous to accept. The visit would give him a chance to look over her home and judge whether or not it was secure enough.

"I'd love to come to your house for supper, Danny," he said. "How about if I bring some ice cream for dessert? What flavor do you like?"

"We don't eat sweets," Lindy blurted, her cheeks red, her eyes widening more by the second.

"Okay. Then I'll bring dill-pickle-flavored," Thad gibed. To his delight, Danny started to laugh so heartily he got short of breath and tears filled his eyes.

Judging by the incredulity on Lindy's face, it

had been a long time since she'd seen her son express that much unbridled amusement.

She finally recovered her composure. "All right. Please join us for supper, Mr. Pearson. And you don't have to bring pickle ice cream. I suppose we can eat normal flavors once in a while without getting too many cavities."

"Chocolate okay?"

She didn't have time to comment before the office phone rang and she slipped into her formal persona to answer. "Pearson Products. How may I help you?"

Thad and Danny watched her grow pale, then reach for the edge of the desk to steady herself.

"What? That's impossible."

Thad didn't know what was being said by the other party to the call but he could tell enough to cause him to reach for the receiver. Instead of balking, Lindy relinquished it to him.

"This is Thad Pearson. Is there something I can do for you?"

"Our business is with Mrs. Southerland."

"Who has just passed your call to me. Now what's going on? She looks like you just told her somebody died."

"Mrs. Southerland has not kept up with her mortgage payments since before Mr. Southerland passed away and there was no insurance on the account to pay off the loan in case of the death of either party. Therefore, she's seriously in default."

"What's that supposed to mean? In plain English."

"According to the acceleration clause in her contract, we can assess late fees as well as require that the loan be paid in full to avoid foreclosure. Our records show that she is six months in arrears as well as owing substantial penalties and processing fees."

"That's impossible. She paid off that loan right after she got her husband's life insurance settlement." Thad looked to Lindy for confirmation and saw her nodding rapidly.

"Not according to our records. Since she has chosen to ignore our letters, I'm afraid we have been forced to begin foreclosure proceedings."

"Hold on. Let me speak to your supervisor."

"I am the supervisor," the harsh female voice insisted. "I'm truly sorry for Mrs. Southerland's situation but it's out of my hands now. We've already filed a 'Notice of Default' with the county clerk's office. This is merely a courtesy call."

"Wait a minute. How did you get this number?" Thad's grip on the phone tightened. "Well?"

"Mrs. Southerland left it as a secondary contact when she called our Atlanta branch earlier today. We've been trying to reach her at home for weeks with no success. If she had not telephoned us this morning to report a so-called theft of funds we would have had to settle for a registered letter."

"You're saying you've phoned her at home?" Once again his eyes met Lindy's. There was no detectable deceit in her expression, only confusion. She shook her head adamantly.

Her scowl deepened as she mouthed, "No."

"Okay, assuming you're just mixed up about all this, give me a number where I can reach you. We'll look into the situation and call you back."

"Calling me won't be necessary. If you disagree with our findings you're welcome to write a letter to the State Banking Department and lodge a formal complaint. If your complaint is valid they may launch an investigation."

"How long can that take?"

"I really can't say."

"All right. We'll be in touch."

He ended the call, sat down at his desk and slid his keyboard closer. There were a lot of things a savvy person could learn with the right connections and he counted himself among the best. Anything a hacker could hide, he could uncover.

He sensed Lindy leaning closer to peer over his shoulder as she said, "That must have been a crank call. I checked into everything I owed right after— well, you know when—and the only debt outstanding was for the mortgage. I took care of that months ago. There's no way I can be in arrears."

"Do you have receipts? Canceled checks?"

"No. I did everything electronically. That's the way Ben always handled our bills."

As Thad typed he noticed that Danny had reverted to his earlier shyness and was clinging to his mother. It didn't take much to set back his healing, did it? Thad wasn't surprised. The simplest memory or most innocent incident might be enough to trigger his own PTSD and unless he missed his guess, this seven-year-old was suffering from similar emotional damage.

Had Lindy taken the child to the right kind of doctors after his trauma? Did he dare ask?

Later, he reasoned. There would be plenty of time to quiz her about her son as they worked together. The last thing he wanted to do was make her mad enough to quit, at least not until he'd sorted out the mess she was in.

Frustrated, he leaned back and shook his head slowly, thoughtfully. "It doesn't look good, Lindy. I can't tell how far the hackers got yet but one thing is certain. They've totally corrupted your accounts to make it look as if you defaulted on the loan the way the bank says."

"So it wasn't just the missing cash we discovered today? It's worse?"

"Much worse."

Without turning around, he laid his hand lightly over hers where it rested on his shoulder and felt her trembling. Thad didn't blame her. His own finances were in turmoil, thanks to having to keep the business afloat while he tried to pick up the pieces of his brother's estate, but his money problems paled in comparison to what someone had done to Lindy.

He sighed. "Look, we'll figure it out. I'll work on it until I do. The important thing is not to panic. This can't all have happened as a result of last night's burglary. It has to have been in the works longer than that. This plan is sophisticated. Complicated. Somebody went to an awful lot of trouble to ruin your credit."

"Why me? I haven't hurt anyone or stolen anything. I've never even had a parking ticket."

"Then you should have called the police the minute you had a reason to," Thad said flatly. "Doing it now will look suspicious."

"It doesn't matter because I'm not calling them."

One dark eyebrow arched and he stared up at her. "Why not? There's no way to tell if this mortgage mix-up is connected to the thugs who threatened you to keep quiet last night."

She met his gaze boldly. "Do *you* think it's separate?"

"No," he admitted quietly, worried about Danny's mental stress as much as Lindy's. "I think you're in the crosshairs of some broad-reaching scheme you have no idea about and everything that's been happening to you goes with it. There. Satisfied?"

Though she did nod, Thad was sorry he'd been so abrupt. The woman was in way over her head. For that matter, it was starting to look as if he was, too, by making the decision to help her, but he wasn't about to throw in the towel. No, sir. When a marine was given an assignment, he carried it out no matter the hardships.

At its heart, this task was no different than combat. They—he and Lindy—were facing an unidentifiable enemy whose methods were hidden and whose tentacles of influence reached far beyond what was visible.

The menace was real. Very real. And he was going to protect her. No matter what it took.

FIVE

Lindy had wanted to start home ahead of her new boss so she could begin cooking but he wouldn't hear of it. She understood his evident concern because she shared it, she just didn't want Danny to sense her uneasiness.

She'd left some of the food she'd bought in the fridge at work so Danny would have after-school snacks. The rest she intended to carry into the house herself. As long as she still *had* a house, that is. The notion that someone could have infiltrated her bank accounts and made her credit look so appalling had shaken her to the core.

Could they actually cause her to lose her beautiful home? Certainly not that easily. Suppose she and Thad managed to thwart that plan as he'd suggested they could? What else might her enemies try next? She didn't even want to think about the possibilities.

"Grab your backpack and don't forget your jacket," she called to her son. "I'll bring the groceries."

Before she could open the trunk of her car and pick up the few remaining plastic sacks, Thad appeared at her elbow. "Fancy place you have here. It looks practically new."

"I'm not sure when it was built. I do know it's newer than the other houses on this street. The yard was a mess when we moved in but I happen to like gardening. Everything will be prettier later in the spring when my flowers start to bloom."

"I'm amazed you can keep it up so well by yourself."

"I manage." She started to gather the plastic grocery sacks.

"I'll get those for you," Thad said pleasantly.

"I can do it."

"I know you can. Humor me. I feel guilty enough letting Danny talk you into feeding me. At least let me pitch in a little."

"Okay." Lindy backed off. Considering the trying day she'd had, what she really wanted to do was take an aspirin, kick back and relax, not prepare a fancy meal for someone she barely knew. Therefore, if Thad wanted to help, she'd let him.

Fisting her key ring, she led the way to the side porch and unlocked the door. Danny burst in and took off at a run. His small feet hammered the stairs as he climbed.

"You can put those bags on the kitchen table," Lindy said, thankful she'd taken the time to load the dishwasher instead of leaving dirty glasses and plates stacked in the sink. Maintaining a routine was comforting, to her and to Danny, so she always made an effort to keep things the same.

A terrified squeal of "Maaa-ma!" echoed down the stairwell.

Lindy froze. Glanced at Thad. Saw recognition dawn as her own mind wrapped itself around the shout.

If she hadn't moved a split second faster than Thad did, they might have collided trying to climb the stairs at the same time.

"Danny!" Lindy shouted. "What's wrong?"

"My room," the child yelled, sticking his head out the open door so she could see his incredulous expression. "Somebody trashed my room."

She slewed around the newel post at the top of the stairs and sensed Thad right behind her as she pivoted.

In seconds they were at Danny's door. The sight that greeted them was unbelievable. No mess made by a child had ever been this bad.

Lindy held out her arms to her distressed son and he flew into her embrace. "I'm so sorry, honey."

"Whoa," Thad said. "I don't suppose it looked like this when he left this morning."

"Of course not. Danny always makes his bed and puts his toys on the shelf or in his closet before he goes to school."

"Okay, if you say so. Personally, my room used to be almost this messy when I was a kid." He caught her eye and arched an eyebrow. "Anybody you want to call to report this?"

She knew exactly what Thad was asking and the temptation to involve the police was growing stronger by the minute.

"Danny and I can clean it up in no time," Lindy said. "I'll help him right after I make supper."

"Tell you what," Thad said with a shrug. "Show me where you keep the ingredients and I'll cook for all of us tonight. I make a mean spaghetti sauce and anybody can boil water for pasta."

"Don't be ridiculous. I didn't invite you here to put you to work."

He began to smile, and, in spite of the emotional turmoil caused by the scattering of her son's possessions, Lindy felt her spirits lift.

"Actually," he drawled, grinning, "you didn't invite me at all. Danny did. You just went along with it because you were too polite to tell me no."

He held up a hand to stop her when she opened her mouth to rebut his statement. "The first thing we're all going to do is go over this house room by room, closet by closet, starting up here, and make sure this is all that was messed with. Then you can give me a quick tour of the downstairs before I get to work."

Although she knew he was only being sensible,

Lindy fisted her hands on her hips and faced him. "Are you always this bossy?"

"Yes. Especially when I know I'm right." The grin widened. "You know I am, too."

"Unfortunately, I do." Sweeping her arm in the direction of the hall she said, "After you, Mr. Pearson."

"I don't suppose you'd like to call me Thad."

"Considering the way you've been ordering me around, I feel more like I should salute and call you *Sir*."

"I've been known to answer to Sergeant," Thad said, sobering, "but I'd rather we stuck to civilian titles if you don't mind."

Taken aback by his swift change of mood, Lindy remembered what Samantha had told her about Thad's medical discharge and wished mightily she had not brought up the military.

"Sorry, *Thad*," she said. "It was just that the way you were barking orders you reminded me of a soldier. I suppose that's natural."

"I suppose it is. Once a marine, always a marine, as they say."

He turned and started on his rounds, stopping to open the linen closet and then inspect a bedroom and bath.

"My husband's home office was in this bedroom," Lindy said, pausing at the next door. "If they were going to bother any room it should have been this one."

"Unless Danny's was hit to distract us. Wait here while I check."

Obeying, Lindy subdued a shudder. When someone had picked on her son they had crossed an invisible line and she was growing more convinced by the minute that she must do something about it.

Lindy watched Thad continuing his search. She had not ventured into that particular room, except to accompany some men from Ben's firm, since his untimely death.

"What about the desk?" Thad asked. "Would you know if anything is missing?"

She shook her head and sighed. "Probably not. I wasn't involved in my husband's business. A few of the partners in the investment company he worked for stopped by and I let them have whatever they wanted after the police and the DEA were through, but that's been months ago. If there had been anything important to find, either those men or the investigators would surely have taken it."

"If they knew what they were looking for," Thad said. "What about his computer?"

"Drug Enforcement confiscated his laptop and a backup hard drive."

"Is there any other computer in the house?"

Backing away so Thad could continue to precede her down the hall, Lindy said, "There's mine, downstairs, but I only use it for email, paying bills and things like that. Oh, and Danny has a little one his dad gave him to play games on."

"Does it have much memory?"

"Only enough to load some simple games, I guess. It's pretty small."

Hearing Thad chuckle softly she frowned at him. "What's so funny?"

"Even the most rudimentary computer these days has more memory than the vehicles that NASA first sent into space. So do smart phones. Size is relative."

"You've made your point. Tell you what. There's nothing in Danny's room that won't wait. How about we all pitch in and make supper together?"

The broad smile that lit Thad's handsome face warmed her heart. When he turned that smile on her son and she saw the gentleness in his expression, her heart was more than warmed. It was jubilant.

This kind of interaction was what she'd hoped for. The problem was, she didn't want Danny to get too attached to any man and then be disappointed the way they'd both been before.

Lindy's fertile mind began to imagine scenarios in which Thad played the villain. He had not given her any reason to see him that way but that didn't matter. He was too good to be true. Too caring. Too good-looking. Too easy to like.

Perhaps she'd become jaded via her bad marriage and was painting everyone with the same broad brush but she couldn't help herself. After a betrayal like Ben's, it was very hard to trust anyone, especially strangers. And that's what Thad Pearson really was.

She took a deep breath and forced herself to reflect on the circumstances that had brought them together. A simple, accidental meeting had led to too much, too fast, to suit her. Chances were the ex-marine was on the up-and-up, yet it did seem awfully strange that he had managed to be in exactly the right places when she'd needed him. If she'd been reading a mystery novel, she'd have doubted that such handy coincidences could have occurred the way they had without a sinister plot behind them.

So, what should she do now? Lindy wondered. In her vivid imaginings she saw two choices: praise God for bringing Thad into her life to help her, or throw him out and bolt the door so he couldn't get back in.

The latter would have been easier except for the fact that she really needed her job—and his help on the computer. That should have been enough to make her believe the poor guy was honest. And it was. Sort of.

She would have liked it better if she'd been able to fully convince herself that Thad wasn't far too good to be true.

It didn't take a genius to tell that Lindy remained shaken up. She put on a happy face for Danny and tried to act relaxed but Thad suspected that the slightest unusual noise would send her right through the roof.

He busied himself at the stove, stirring the bubbling tomato sauce while Danny set the rectangular table in one corner of the kitchen and Lindy made a salad. Being there with the two of them almost made him feel normal again.

Humph. That would be the day. The closest he'd ever come to feeling as if he was a part of a real family was when he'd visited Rob and Ellen and played with their kids.

He shuddered at the thought that those innocent children might have perished in the same fire that took their parents' lives.

"Are you all right?" Lindy asked.

"Fine. Why?"

"I thought I saw you shiver."

Shivering didn't even begin to cover his tenuous emotional state, Thad mused. If he wasn't careful, he'd slip over the edge into the kinds of intense memories that sometimes triggered a relapse of his

PTSD. He could not let that happen. Especially not when an already fragile child was present.

Thad's everyday calm demeanor wasn't an act. What he was doing was managing his thoughts enough to redirect them and temper the irrational fear and survivor's guilt that sometimes flowed through him no matter what mind games he played with himself.

"I'm fine. Just thinking about your situation and wondering how I can make your house safer." *While you still have a house,* he added to himself.

"That's hardly your problem," Lindy said flatly. "If I've learned anything in the past six months, it's to face one day at a time. This is the second break-in we've had and I've decided it's time I reported the crimes to the sheriff."

Thad couldn't help grinning. "*Now* you're talking sense."

"I hope so. I really do." She carried the salad bowl to the table, then went to the refrigerator and returned with bottled dressing. "Since nobody left any threats this time, maybe the two incidents aren't connected."

"And maybe pigs can fly," he quipped.

When Danny piped up with, "Really? *Can* they?" it made both adults chuckle.

"No, honey. Mr. Pearson was just joking."

Thad figured it was time to lighten the mood

even more so he drawled, "If their wings were big enough, I think it might be possible."

It pleased him to hear Danny giggle. "Pigs don't have wings. I saw some when Mom took me to the county fair."

"Okay, if you say so," Thad replied with a wide grin.

He noticed that Lindy was laughing, too, and, before he could stop himself, his amusement and sense of belonging caused him to wink at her. He didn't mean anything by it, it just happened. At least he thought it did. Truth to tell, he wasn't sure why he'd done it and judging by her astonished expression she hadn't expected it, either.

Blushing, he cleared his throat. "Um, sorry about that. I didn't mean…"

To his relief she quickly recovered her composure, smiled and said, "No offense taken. I sometimes get something in my eye and have to blink it out, too."

The ensuing silence in the small kitchen was so noticeable that everyone paused. Danny looked first to his mother, then to Thad.

That caused Thad to glance over at Lindy. The moment her eyes met his and he saw the lively twinkle in them, he knew they were sharing and enjoying a private moment just the way Rob and Ellen often had.

Such happenings were so foreign to Thad he

became extremely ill at ease. Clearing his throat he found his voice and said, "Well, then, now that we know we don't have to worry about seeing pigs roosting in trees, I guess we can relax and enjoy dinner."

"Supper," Danny corrected.

"Right. Supper it is. I'll drain the pasta and get this all stirred together."

"Ewww. That's not how you do it," the boy insisted.

Lindy stepped up. "We usually serve the sauce separately. I'll get a couple big bowls."

Leaning down, she opened one of the oak cupboards beneath the far end of the granite countertop and peered inside.

Thad paid little attention until she suddenly shrieked and jumped back.

He dropped the stirring spoon into the pot and crossed to her in three long strides, cupping her shoulders and steadying her. "What is it? What happened?"

Lindy's mouth opened but no sound escaped. She pointed.

Stepping in front of her, Thad had to bend low to see what she'd found so frightening. Once he laid eyes on the problem he understood perfectly. The dirty-brown-colored thing was nearly as big as a rolled-up dish towel. It was also quite dead.

"Don't worry. That rat can't hurt you. I'll dispose of it."

"We've never had a rodent problem in this house. Not even a stray mouse." Her voice cracked. "Somebody had to put that there."

"You didn't actually touch it, did you?"

"No."

"Good." Thad wasn't about to pick up the carcass barehanded. He looked under the sink for a pair of rubber gloves and settled for a discarded plastic grocery sack instead.

Slipping his hand inside the bag, he grasped the body, then simply inverted the bag so the dead vermin was inside before he let go and held the sack closed by fisting it at the top. He might have argued with Lindy's snap judgment about its origin if he had not spotted something odd tied to the hairless tail.

"I'll go drop this into the back of my truck so it'll be safe until the authorities get here. Don't touch anything in that cabinet, not even to close the door. Understand?"

Lindy had backed all the way across the kitchen with her little boy as if the wild animal was still alive and about to attack them. "Why not? The whole kitchen needs to be disinfected and everything stored in that cupboard has to be sterilized."

"Later," Thad said flatly. "Do that after the sheriff and his deputies have been here and dusted for prints." Staring at her, willing her to act, he added, "Are you going to call them now or am I?"

To his relief, Lindy replied, "I will."

SIX

County Sheriff Harlan Allgood responded to the call himself and parked at the curb in front of Lindy's house.

She watched him swing his ample bulk out of the black-and-white, hitch up his holster and square his hat on his head. Like ninety-nine percent of the men in the rural South, he wore a ball cap, only his was emblazoned with *Fulton County Sheriff* instead of the usual sports team logos or hunting and fishing scenes.

Lindy wasn't sure Thad knew Harlan until she saw the men greet each other at the door and shake hands amiably.

"It's over there. In the bed of my truck," Thad said, stepping outside to lead the way.

Lindy stayed back with Danny and let the men poke around the animal on their own. She wasn't usually the squeamish type. She liked all creatures, wild or domestic. But dead ones in her kitchen were a different story.

They had decided to put off eating while they waited for the sheriff. Right now, Lindy wondered if she'd ever want to dine in her cozy kitchen again, even after she'd sanitized it completely.

"Did you see this, Miz Southerland?" Harlan called.

"Unfortunately. I was the one who found it."

"I mean this note." The sheriff had donned latex gloves and was working on something that now lay on the open tailgate of Thad's truck.

"Note?"

"Yep. I'll have to take it with me as evidence but I thought maybe you could shed a little light on it."

"Okay. I'll try."

Leading her son to keep him close, she tried to put on a brave front as they descended the front porch steps.

Danny let go of her hand and reached for Thad's as soon as they drew near enough. Not only did his action surprise Lindy, it hurt her feelings a little. She had gotten so used to being the only person Danny relied upon that it was unsettling to see him gravitate to Thad.

Setting aside that concern, she leaned over to look at a piece of paper. The sheriff had trained a flashlight on it and was securing one edge with gloved fingers. It had been folded multiple times and then crinkled down the middle as if cinched by the string she could see still attached to the animal.

Incredulous, Lindy stared. Her jaw gaped. The leaf from a notepad was engraved with Ben's former company's logo. Worse, the scrawl was familiar. She would have recognized her late husband's handwriting anywhere. Seeing this was like receiving a message from the grave!

"That can't be," she said, her voice faltering. "It...it looks like Ben wrote that."

She felt a supporting arm around her shoulders and leaned into Thad without thinking.

"It's obviously somebody's idea of a bad joke," he said. "They must have gotten hold of an old memo and are trying to scare you with it."

"Well, it worked," she said wryly. "Look at what it says, how well it fits this situation. Ben is talking about handling money and keeping his mouth shut because of threats against him. And his family. Where in the world could that have come from?"

The sheriff was shaking his head and shrugging as he slipped the note into a plastic sleeve to preserve it. "No telling. What do you suppose he meant when he mentioned secret bank accounts?"

"How should *I* know? I can't even keep my own finances straight." Thad's grip tightened as her voice rose. "My husband didn't share his business dealings with me. Ever."

"Sorry," Harlan said. "I had to ask. So, do you want me to dust the area where you found your furry little buddy or not?"

"Dust my whole house if it will help," Lindy said. "I've just about had it with all these stupid attacks."

"Attacks?" She watched the older man's bushy eyebrows arching. "Am I missing something here?"

"Yes," Lindy admitted ruefully. "This is only the latest in a series of recent problems I've had. Maybe you'd better come in for a cup of coffee while I explain everything. We were about to eat supper when we found that—that *thing* in the cupboard. You're welcome to join us for a plate of spaghetti if you like."

Harlan grinned. "Thanks—as long as you keep it in a different part of the kitchen than where you found this messenger."

"It's safe on the stove. The rest of my food is separate, too. It's just the idea of that *thing* being in one of my storage cupboards that turns my stomach."

"We know he didn't get there on his own," Thad volunteered. "The rest of the house should be clean."

"Unless whoever left that carcass decided that one message wasn't enough." Lindy shivered. "I don't even want to think about finding any more."

But she would think about it, which was obviously the whole point. Her nemesis was trying to unhinge her and he was doing a pretty good job of it, too. She would not, could not, let him win.

"They won't scare me as much the next time, if there is a next time," Lindy vowed.

Harlan gave her a sincere, "Atta girl."

She might have objected to being called a *girl* if she hadn't known he came from a generation that thought of any woman as a girl, even those old enough to be grandmothers. Many ladies in Serenity were addressed as *Miss* This or *Miss* That rather than simply called by their given names. It was a charming Southern custom that countless generations had grown up with.

She'd thought that Danny would grow up with it, too. Was she going to have to flee Serenity in order to protect her son and see to it that he had a normal childhood?

She certainly hoped not. Now that Ben was gone, she was really beginning to feel as if she belonged in the small, rural community. Leaving it would mean bidding her friends a permanent goodbye. If she didn't want her enemies to follow her, she knew she'd have to cut all ties. Completely.

Was it possible to hide that well on her own? she wondered. Probably not. Even people in the Federal Witness Protection Program were revealed every now and then. Since she would still be tied to a bank account which was practically her sole support, there was no way she'd be able to just vanish.

And when that money was gone? When Ben no longer had any more wages or commissions due him? If she could have sold the house and taken those profits with her, it might have been enough to finance a fresh start. Now that title to the property was also in limbo she'd lost that option.

Thinking about leaving her new job and the boss who had already become such an integral part of her life, Lindy felt a sense of sadness wash over her like icy winter rain.

It chilled her to the bone in seconds and helped strengthen her resolve. She and Danny were not going anywhere. This was their home. They were *not* going to be driven from it by any threats, real or imagined.

"I'll want you to check Danny's room, too," she told the portly sheriff as he stripped off his gloves and dropped them into a separate plastic bag. "Somebody ransacked it while we were gone today."

"Can you tell if anything was taken?" he asked.

"The way it looks now we can't even tell if there's still a rug on the floor," Lindy said wryly. "Whoever tore it apart did a bang-up job."

"Okay." He reached for the radio clipped to his belt and requested backup.

When he was finished speaking he smiled. "Now, Miz Southerland, how about that meal and maybe a quick cup of coffee while you tell me everything that's happened, right from the beginning."

Although Lindy grimaced as she led the way back inside, she knew it was time to come clean. There was only so much she—and Thad—could do on their own and it wasn't smart to exclude the professionals like Harlan and his officers.

"We're not sure exactly when somebody started harassing me," she began. "The first inkling I had was when I surprised a couple prowlers in the house. Danny and I hid behind the sofa until they left."

As she had suspected, Harlan did not receive her opening remarks well. His brow knit and she could see the muscles in his jaw clenching. If he had been her father rather than the sheriff, she imagined he'd have been yelling by then.

In retrospect, it was no surprise that she'd married Ben. He had been a lot like her dad with a temper to match. The major difference between them was that her father had not been physically abusive even on his worst day. With Ben, the abuse had started about a year before he'd been killed. The reason he had changed so drastically still eluded her, although she surmised it had had something to do with his involvement with criminals.

Fixing a dish of spaghetti for herself and her hungry child while the others helped themselves,

Lindy dreaded the interrogation she knew was coming. As Thad had told her, the fact that she hadn't reported the attacks immediately made her look as if she was hiding something.

If she could have found the proper words, she might have tried to explain how, in spite of herself, she couldn't help blaming her husband's demise on the way the authorities had stormed the cabin where she, Danny and Samantha were being held hostage six months before. Ben had died in the ensuing shoot-out. Logically, she knew it wasn't the police's fault. They'd done their best, and really, it was a marvel they hadn't *all* been killed.

For that, she supposed she should have thanked God, yet she was still struggling to do so. Perhaps returning to church, as Samantha had urged, would help her as well as Danny. It couldn't hurt. The way Lindy saw it, her biggest problem was the fact that she'd been unable to properly forgive any of the parties involved at that time, particularly her late husband.

In her deepest heart she knew there was one far more important fact, a weakness she constantly struggled to overcome, both consciously and subconsciously.

She was angry at God.

Thad sat patiently at the dining room table with the others and listened while Lindy laid out the events of the past few days. The sheriff took notes between forkfuls of food. Thad didn't add anything or argue with her conclusions until she'd finished speaking.

"There's one more problem," he interjected soberly. "Somebody has tried to destroy Ms. Southerland's credit. They've tapped into her bank accounts and messed up the record that she'd paid off the mortgage on this house."

Harlan's left eyebrow arched. "When did this happen?"

"I got a call from my bank in Atlanta today," Lindy said. "I'm pretty sure we can iron out those difficulties. It has to be a clerical error."

"You think so?" He took a sip from his coffee mug and tilted his head for emphasis. "Sounds to me like it's all cut from the same cloth."

Lindy scowled back at him. "How can it be? I didn't do anything wrong. I don't understand who can possibly be trying to ruin me."

"You were Ben Southerland's wife. Maybe that's enough."

Thad leaned forward, elbows on the table and stared at her. "Think. There must be something. Anything. You're sure Ben never told you about what he was doing besides being an normal investment counselor?"

"Not a word. Lots of people who didn't know us well might assume he and I were confidants simply because we were married, but we weren't. Ben was adamant that I keep my nose out of his business affairs. I only saw him discussing his work once."

"When? Where?"

"It was about a year ago. Near Little Rock. I happened to be in the car when Ben got out to meet with some men who were strangers to me. They all looked very serious, even angry, but I couldn't hear a thing they were saying. Cross my heart."

"Well, somebody must think you know more than that," Harlan said flatly. He wiped his mouth with his napkin, laid it aside, then stood and hitched up his utility belt and holster. "Thanks for supper. I'll take care of the fingerprint work out in the kitchen. When my deputy, Adelaide Crowe, gets here you can take her into the boy's room and show her what was moved."

Thad also stood. "Thank *you,* Sheriff. I know we haven't always seen eye to eye. I'm glad to see you taking all this seriously."

The sheriff huffed. "It's serious as a dead rat, son. I was afraid something like this might happen after the set-to in the woods last year, but I figured it had blown over by now."

"Meaning?"

"Meaning, we caught the getaway driver. And the two bag men who did the kidnapping were killed in the raid on their hideout. Trouble is, we never did manage to track down any bigger fish. That means they're still out there. And it's beginnin' to look like Miz Southerland has their attention."

"What're you going to do about it?" Thad asked.

"Start by takin' prints and gatherin' clues, unless you two happen to know more than you're tellin' me. You sure did take your time tellin' me this much."

Thad's gaze met Lindy's and he saw an expression of contrition. Well, that fit. She had ignored his suggestions to contact the sheriff immediately and if he hadn't been there to make the call after her fender bender, that incident wouldn't be on the record, either.

"You do remember about the so-called accident this morning, don't you?" Thad prodded.

"Yep. We took scrapings from the mashed fender and sent 'em off. No telling how long the lab will take before we get the results back. So far, this isn't real high priority."

"Then tie it to the original case you were just talking about and make it high priority," Thad insisted.

"All in due time." The older man absently scratched his chin. "Let's put a few more facts together before we jump to conclusions."

Lindy had opened her mouth as if she wanted

to say something before abruptly turning away. Thad could tell she was frustrated and more than a little upset. He didn't blame her. She'd assumed she'd put the troubles of her past behind her and now the sheriff was suggesting otherwise.

The headlights of another vehicle illuminated the driveway and shone through the windows briefly.

"That'll be Adelaide," Harlan said, heading for the door. "I'll go make sure she brings an evidence kit in with her."

As soon as he was gone, Thad looked to Lindy. "He's just doing his job, you know."

"I know."

There was enough resignation and sorrow in her tone to make Thad's gut twist. "I wish there was something I could do for you right now."

When she raised her gaze to meet his, smiled slightly and said, "Just being here with us is enough," he felt more than touched. He felt connected.

What they would decide to do later was up in the air but he knew he'd agree to pretty much anything she suggested. The important thing was to keep her and Danny safe. If he had to sleep in his truck in her driveway to do that, he would.

Lindy was embarrassed to admit how much she desired Thad's company. He must think she was either crazy or the clingiest woman in the state of Arkansas. They hardly knew each other, yet she had been absolutely honest when she'd told him that she was glad he was there. In the space of a single day, a stranger had become her anchor, her shelter from whatever or whoever wanted to harm her.

That whole premise was preposterous. It was also true. Like it or not, she and her son needed the protection of the man she had been formally introduced to barely ten hours ago. If she had not been directly involved in the entire situation she would not have believed it was possible, let alone probable.

Her head was spinning with wild speculation. She closed her eyes for a moment and felt Thad's hand gently cup her elbow.

"You okay?"

"No," Lindy said quietly. "I was just wondering if we'll ever be okay again."

"Of course you will." He directed her toward the hallway. "You and Danny go wait outside his room."

"What about these dirty dishes? I suppose I should leave them for now."

"Probably. I'll stick the leftovers in the fridge for you so they don't spoil, then bring the deputy up."

Shaking her head, Lindy stood firm. "No. This

is my house. I'll deal with her myself." A smile twitched at the corners of her mouth as she looked at her son. "Danny and I will help the deputy go over his things and then we'll straighten everything up."

"You're sure?"

"I'm sure." The smile grew and she focused on her handsome benefactor. "You've done more than enough already. Thank you for everything."

"That sounds like an invitation to leave."

The crestfallen look on Thad's face was touching. "No way, mister. Unless you feel like running to keep from becoming more involved in my crazy life, I'd love to have you stick around. I don't know how long all this is going to take but I really would like company."

"*I'm* here," the boy piped up.

Lindy tousled his hair. "And I don't know what I'd do without you. I just meant that it's good to have a grown-up friend here, too."

"Yeah," the child answered with a wide grin. "He's pretty cool."

"There. See?" Lindy told Thad. "You have the approval of the man of the house."

"That's a heavy burden for such small shoulders," Thad said, speaking aside.

Although Lindy agreed, she didn't think this was the right time or place to discuss family dynamics. Letting Danny feel important had been the suggestion of his pediatrician right after the fatal shooting and the child acted proud of his new role.

The way she had envisioned the future, she and Danny would be all the family either of them needed. They had always been close and since Ben's death their bond had strengthened even more. The little boy was her life. She would devote herself to him and make up for the rocky start he'd gotten because of her poor choices.

And if Danny needed a male role model the way Thad had insisted? That was easy. She'd just continue to cultivate the friendship that was beginning to blossom between her and the ex-marine. If that relationship didn't work out, she'd find others to mentor her son.

In the back of her mind was the niggling suspicion that she was personally attracted to her new boss but she tamped down that notion. It was silly to even imagine herself getting involved with another man.

Lindy wasn't the type to have a fling or settle for less than complete commitment. She might not be attending church at present but her morals were straight out of the Bible. That was one of the ways Ben had found to coerce her. Whenever he had wanted total control, he had reminded her that she was commanded to be submissive and dedicated only to him.

She huffed in disgust. It had taken much soul-searching and poring over scripture for her to realize she was being manipulated. By the time she'd learned what the Bible really meant, it had been too late. She had already alienated the few distant relatives remaining on her side of the family and had also become a widow.

And thankful to be free, Lindy added with more than a modicum of guilt. She was certain it must be a sin to thank God for her freedom even though she would never have wished Ben dead.

Still, when she remembered her past life with that man, she couldn't help feeling that she had narrowly escaped a fate worse than death.

And so had her innocent son.

But had they really escaped after all? With Ben dead, Lindy had hoped to leave the past in the past. But someone seemed determined to pull her and her son back into danger again.

SEVEN

It was nearly midnight by the time the sheriff and his deputy finished gathering evidence.

Thad ventured upstairs after Harlan was done in the kitchen and discovered that Danny had fallen asleep in his mother's arms.

Deputy Adelaide Crowe had packaged up the results of her search of the boy's room and was leaving, too.

Lindy brightened visibly when she saw Thad in the doorway. "My helper conked out."

"He looks heavy. Here. Let me take him for you."

"It's okay. Really."

"I know, I know. You can do it. But wouldn't you like a rest?"

She managed a shrug. "Yes. This kid weighs a ton. I know he's gained at least five pounds in the past few months. His pediatrician says he's a lot healthier for it."

"He didn't eat well when his father was at the same table, right?"

"How did you know?"

Thad thought of saying, *Been there, done that,* but settled for "That's typical."

"I suppose so. We were both pretty careful to keep from antagonizing Ben. He was far too stern, especially about table manners and things like that. Nobody's perfect, especially not kids."

Thad opened his arms and Lindy carefully passed the groggy child to him. "I take it you tried to be the perfect wife."

She smiled thinly. "I *was* the perfect wife. I just couldn't convince my husband of it."

That brought a wider smile, especially when Thad chuckled softly. "*I* believe you. Anybody who's willing to take on the job of straightening up my office deserves a gold medal in my book."

Yawning behind her hand, Lindy blinked. "It must be really late. I'm sorry to have kept you so long."

"No sweat." The bed was still piled with toys and now dusted with gray fingerprint powder, as well. "Where do you want me to put him? It's obvious he can't sleep there until you've washed everything, even the blankets."

"I see that." She yawned again. "Sorry. I guess you should take him to my room."

"Where will you sleep?"

"That's the least of my worries right now. I may be exhausted but I'm not a bit sleepy."

Thad didn't bother to argue. He wasn't sure what he was going to do from this point on and was waiting for more clues from her. If he volunteered to stay over, she'd probably think he was making inappropriate advances, yet, if he walked away, there was no telling what calamity might befall this little family.

Together, he and Lindy settled the child on her bed and covered him with a crocheted afghan after removing his shoes and socks. The boy looked so tiny lying in the middle of that wide bed. It made him seem even more lost than Thad knew he was.

Lindy led the way out of the room. Night-lights glowed from wall plugs up and down the hall, giving the passage a surreal aspect.

As Thad glanced her way, he was impressed by the jut of her chin and the sureness of her steps. She had recovered a lot of self-confidence in the time she and the female deputy had been in Danny's room.

"That's what we should have done," Thad murmured.

"What is?"

"Ask Deputy Crowe to stay with you tonight so wouldn't have to worry."

"I'm not your problem. I'll lock the doors and check all the windows after you leave, I promise."

The ridiculousness of her assurance upset him. "Somebody got in before. More than once. What makes you think a simple lock will keep them out if they decide to pay you another visit?"

Lindy's head snapped around and her mouth opened but she failed to come up with a rebuttal. Clearly, she had been having similar unsettling thoughts.

"What do you suggest?" Her eyebrows arched.

"I don't know." Thad held out his hands, palms toward her. "I'm not trying to talk you into letting me sleep here. I know preserving your good reputation is important. But I don't intend to just drive away and leave you unprotected." He raked his fingers through his short hair. "I can sleep in my truck in your driveway."

"Don't be silly. It's cold out there."

"So, loan me a blanket."

Waiting for an answer, he could sense the wheels turning in her brain. If she came up with a viable alternative, she was a lot smarter than he was because he'd been mulling that problem over for hours and hadn't been able to think of anything else.

Finally Lindy nodded, whirled and left him standing in the middle of the living room. In seconds she had returned with blankets and a pillow

"Okay," she said, "This is only for one night,

though. Tomorrow I'll either get better locks on the doors and install an alarm—or hire a bodyguard."

Thad wondered where she thought she'd get enough money to afford either but kept his ideas to himself. One day at a time would have to suffice. That sensible attitude had sustained him on the field of battle and it would do the same here.

Instead of ushering him out immediately as he'd expected, Lindy laid the stack of bedding on the end of the sofa, plunked down next to it with a deep sigh and kicked off her shoes.

"Whew. I don't think I've ever been this tired in my whole life."

"It has been a long day."

That comment made her smile again. "You *think?*"

He chuckled and made himself comfortable in a leather upholstered recliner that matched part of the checkered pattern in the couch. "Yeah. I hope tomorrow is easier on all of us."

"Uh-huh."

"Mind if I go make sure everything is locked up tight for you? I know you said you were going to do it but…"

She waved him away, laid her head back and closed her eyes. "Go. I trust you."

By the time Thad was finished inspecting the entire house and locking the rear and side doors, Lindy had fallen asleep right where she sat.

Unfolding the lighter of the two blankets, he gently draped it over her then stood back. He knew she had to be in her mid-to late twenties but, sitting there with her reddish-gold hair fanned out on the back of the sofa and her lovely face relaxed in slumber, she looked more like a teenager than the mother of a second grader.

Get a grip, Pearson, he told himself. *You know there's no chance of a relationship here. Quit getting distracted.*

That was going to be easier said than done. He and Lindy seemed to be in tune on a level that he had never before experienced and it continued to amaze him. There were times when he felt they shared more than words; they shared feelings and deep, personal convictions.

Thad eased the remaining blanket and the pillow off the armrest and straightened. Once he locked the door and closed it behind him, he'd have no way to get back inside.

Would he need to? Probably not. Considering all the Sheriff's Department activity that had gone on around the house and with his truck still parked in the driveway in plain sight, chances were good that anyone bent on causing more trouble would just go away tonight.

And tomorrow? Or the day after that and the day after that? Thad asked himself. What would he do then?

Walking slowly to the front door and easing it open quietly he made sure that the locking mechanism was engaged before he pulled it shut with a click that sounded much louder in the quiet of the night.

He stood on the porch and scanned the neighborhood. There were a few small outside lights burning by some of the other homes and streetlights illuminated the roadway, but otherwise the whole block was dark. Silent. Apparently deserted.

That was good. It just would have pleased him more to see one or two night owls still up watching TV.

Or even spying on their neighbors, he added cynically. The more nosy eyes that were trained on Lindy, the better.

Sighing, he crossed the neatly mown lawn to his truck, climbed in the passenger side so he'd have more legroom and rolled one window down partway to let in fresh air. This promised to be a long night.

Thad closed his eyes and began to pray silently as he'd learned to do in combat zones.

This time his prayer wasn't for his comrades-in-arms or for himself. It was for the innocent woman and child sleeping alone and vulnerable in that big, expensive house.

He wondered briefly how much Lindy had owed

on a fancy place like that and how he was going to prove she'd paid off the loan.

Also turning that problem over to God, Thad finally dozed off.

They were under fire. Sounds of battle echoed. His eardrums throbbed.

An IED went off beneath the Humvee just ahead in the convoy.

Thad could hear the screams of the wounded and dying.

Seated in the cab of a transport vehicle, Thad rapidly punched the keys on his laptop, searching for information that would give them a safe exit route.

There was none.

They were trapped.

How could this have happened?

Men around him were being hit over and over. Bullets impacting metal sang a dirge.

He threw aside the useless computer, grabbed his rifle and rolled out onto the sand.

Before he could return fire, a bullet tore into him. Astonished, he looked down and saw his life's blood pulsing away.

Distant civilians cried out and shouted angrily. The mob was coming closer and closer. To finish him off for good.

He thought of home. Of peace and safety, then raised his rifle.

* * *

A loud, ringing sound awakened Lindy with a start. It took her several seconds to realize where she was and why she wasn't sleeping in her own bed.

Only two landline phones remained since she now relied mostly on her cell. One was upstairs in Ben's old office and the other was hanging on the kitchen wall. She opted for the closest.

"Hello?" No one spoke. She clutched the receiver tighter and tried again. "Hello?"

She was about to hang up when a gravelly voice said, "We warned you."

Her breath caught. Her pulse hammered. But she forced her voice to sound strong and steady. "Leave me alone."

"Not 'til you start cooperating, lady. We told you no cops. Or else."

Lindy was frightened, yes, but she'd also had just about enough of this ongoing harassment. Anger gave her courage. "What did you expect me to do when I found that dead rat you planted in my kitchen? Huh? You went way too far this time."

The ensuing silence on the other end of the line surprised her. After several seconds, the caller broke the connection with a loud click.

Suddenly weak-kneed, Lindy hung up and leaned against the wall. Whoever had threatened her was obviously watching her house or he wouldn't have known about the sheriff being called. That, alone, was terrifying.

Worse, Thad might be in more danger than either of them had thought when they had agreed he'd sleep in his truck. He'd made a target of himself for whoever was watching them. What she wanted to do was hide inside the house. What she knew she must do, instead, was warn him. But how?

Lindy eyed the telephone. Neither of them had thought to exchange cell numbers before he'd left or she could have called him. By the time she managed to look him up, if she even could, the man who had just threatened her again might have already attacked.

There was only one logical course of action. She had to go out and warn Thad.

She padded barefoot to the bay window that faced the street, pulled back the drapes and peered out. She could see his old truck but it was too dark to tell if anyone was inside it. If he'd already been discovered, he might be injured rather than asleep. Given the telephone threat she'd just received, that was certainly possible.

There was only one way to be sure he was there, was unharmed and stayed safe. She'd have to speak to him in person. The man had already done far more to help her than anyone else ever had. She was not about to let anything bad happen to him simply because she was afraid of the dark.

She did, however, plan to arm herself before she left the house. Casting around for a makeshift weapon, Lindy was at a loss. She didn't even own a baseball bat, let alone a real object intended for defense.

The closest she could come was a garden rake. It wouldn't be easy to wield but she figured it would be better than facing unseen danger empty-handed.

The rake and her other gardening supplies were stored in the garage which was attached to the main house, so, happily, she wouldn't have to venture outside to grab it.

With a flashlight in one hand and the handle of the rake in the other, she eased open her front door, checked to make certain there was no one lurking on the porch or in the yard, then started toward the driveway.

The grass was damp and chilly on her bare feet, making her wish she'd bothered to slip her shoes back on.

Every few seconds she'd pause and listen. Other than distant rumblings from a few cars and an occasional dog barking, the night seemed peaceful. Quiet. Unthreatening.

Lindy had nearly reached her goal when she

heard guttural muttering. Did Thad's truck just move slightly or was her imagination playing tricks on her?

She froze. Watching. Waiting.

There it was again. A man's voice. And he sounded as if he was suffering terribly. Was she too late? Had someone already hurt Thad?

Panicky, she ran the rest of the way. Shining her light through the passenger side window, she saw him. He was fighting, all right, but his eyes were closed and his foe existed only in his troubled dreams.

What should she do? What could she do? If she woke him abruptly, it might be worse than letting him exit the nightmare on his own. It was also foolish to stand there, out in the open, exposed to a real attack. If she did rouse him, it would at least free him from whatever imaginary terror he was battling.

Resolute, Lindy shined the light on her own face so Thad would know it was her, then rapped on the window.

He didn't respond. Whatever night terrors had him in their grip were holding on tight.

The window was open an inch or so at the top so she called his name. "Thad?" Then louder, "Thad! Wake up."

Instead of slowly coming to his senses he reacted as if he were under a real attack and thrust the door open with such force it knocked Lindy backward.

All she had time to do was scream, "No!" before he was lunging for her.

She dropped the rake and flashlight as she fell, trying to ward off the attack by crossing her arms over her face the way she had when Ben had threatened to beat her.

Reality overcame her self-control. She pulled herself into a fetal position and began to sob.

Time stopped.

Gentle hands touched her arm. Lifted her. Calmed her. Gathered her closer and helped her stand.

Thad was speaking but she was too upset to tell what he was saying.

A warm, comforting embrace followed.

Lindy buried her face against his shoulder and struggled to stop crying. She hadn't expected such a vivid reminder of her life as a battered woman and had reacted through habit. She knew that. It was nevertheless terribly embarrassing.

"I'm—I'm so sorry," Lindy managed to say. "I didn't mean to startle you like that." She could feel his hand trembling as he stroked her back through her sweater.

"Did I hurt you?"

"No. Not a bit."

"What are you doing out here?" The question was half grumble, half poignant query.

"The telephone woke me. I couldn't see you in the truck so I came out to make sure you were okay."

"I don't remember what I was dreaming about except that I was back fighting the war. When you startled me, I must have thought…" He pulled her closer. "Oh, Lindy, I'm so sorry."

"I'm fine. Really." Sniffling, she eased away from him. "Does this kind of thing happen to you very often?"

"No. Not anymore. I guess I was just keyed up over everything else and the bad dreams took over." Thad looked down into her upturned face. "Are you sure you're not hurt?"

"Positive." In the dim reflections from the streetlight, she could see moisture glistening on his face and wondered if it was perspiration. Might it be tears, instead? She certainly wasn't going to embarrass him by asking.

"In that case, what in the world were you thinking? Leaving the house was crazy."

"I brought a weapon," she insisted, pointing at the garden tool where it lay on the grass. "And a flashlight. See? They're right there."

He released her, stepped farther back and thrust his hands into his pockets. "Great. What were you going to do, *rake* the bad guys into a nice neat pile and then call the sheriff?"

"No, I was going to hit them with the handle, if you must know. I thought about bringing a big knife from the kitchen but I knew I could never use something like that."

She didn't understand Thad's apparent lack of appreciation for how hard it had been for her to come outside. It might not faze a macho man like him to walk out into the dark when there was a threat of real danger but it had taken a ton of courage for her to do so.

Bending, Lindy scooped up the light and the rake at the same time and backed away with them. She was upset enough to speak her mind.

"Look, Mr. Pearson. I understand you've put yourself out for me and my son and I really do value your efforts, but the guy on the phone sounded as if he was watching the house. I couldn't just sit in there without trying to warn you. Okay?"

"*That's* what the call was about? Why didn't you say so in the first place?" He stood tall and began to scan the deep shadows in the yard. "What did the guy say? Exactly."

"He was upset that the sheriff had been here."

"Half the town probably knows about that already. What else?"

"If you must know, I lost my temper. I told him

that he'd gone too far when he left that horrible creature in my house."

"How did he respond?"

"He didn't. He hung up."

"No argument? No denial?" Thad continued to remain on full alert as he said, "He didn't even laugh or tell you that you'd deserved it?"

"No." Suddenly chilled to the bone, Lindy shivered.

Thad slid his arm around her and started to usher her toward the house. When she looked ahead and noticed that, in her haste, she'd failed to slam the door, she was astounded. Not only was it standing partially open, the inside lights illuminated her error for all to see.

"Good thing we were so close," Thad grumbled. "You practically invited the bad guys to pay you another visit."

"You don't have to remind me. I can see that."

He hustled her through the heavy door and closed it behind them with a bang.

"I hope that didn't wake Danny." Lindy started for the stairs. "I'll go check on him then come back and make coffee, if you'd like."

"Sure." Thad sighed heavily. "I think you and I need to have a talk."

Pausing at the bottom of the staircase, Lindy turned and studied him. "Do you ever have flash-backs during the day?"

"No. It's always when I'm asleep. Right after I got out of the service I bunked with my brother's family—until one of my episodes scared them half to death. That's why I got my own place. Maybe, if I'd still been with Rob and Ellen when the fire started..."

"You'd have died with them," Lindy offered. "I heard there was an explosion first. It was amazing they got the kids out alive."

He sighed noisily. "Yeah. It was. I wish I could have adopted all three of them but, as you just learned the hard way, I'm not fit to be a father."

"Give yourself time," Lindy said gently. "You just need to heal."

"Like you do?"

"I don't know what you mean."

"The way you reacted to my confusion seemed pretty overblown. I know the phone call had you spooked but you practically got hysterical out there."

"You surprised me, that's all."

"Right."

Thad was nodding agreement and his reply indicated the same, yet the look in his eyes contradicted that opinion. The man was too wise, too intuitive to suit her. She did have a lingering problem; one that might forever hurt her.

The trouble was, she had no idea how to find

the kind of peace she craved—for her son's sake as much as for her own.

Just when she thought she'd dealt with the emotional baggage from her abusive marriage, something new happened to trigger her latent fear and almost incapacitate her. Like the events of tonight.

The difference was that this time the hands that had lifted, soothed and comforted her had been kind, gentle. Undemanding.

Lindy closed her eyes for an instant and relived that moment when she'd found unanticipated peace. She could still feel Thad's touch, sense his concern, remember the reassurance she had drawn from his warm embrace.

That was the kind of wordless encouragement she yearned to impart to her son.

And, whether she was willing to openly admit it or not, she wanted the same thing for herself.

EIGHT

Lindy and Thad's late-night, in-depth conversation had been fairly productive. He had fielded a few specific questions regarding his past trauma, keeping his main focus on how he could help her deal with everything that had happened to her, including her husband's murder.

Their situation was pretty ironic, he concluded, since he and Lindy obviously shared enough survivor's guilt to incapacitate a dozen people.

In the end, they had agreed to concentrate on dealing with their present problems and ignore the past as much as possible. He could tell she hated being in the dark about so many things, such as who was harassing her and how far they might eventually go if nobody stopped them. Right now, however, they agreed that they had little choice other than to exercise patience.

Thad had returned to his truck for the balance of that night. The following morning he had followed Lindy when she'd dropped Danny at school on her way to work, beginning a weekday routine that continued unchanged.

Thankfully, there had been no other incidents on subsequent nights, yet Thad still sensed that they were being watched, probably by more than one set of eyes, which was why he had insisted on installing new dead bolts on all her exterior doors.

He could tell Lindy was still dealing with lingering nervousness in spite of her outwardly calm demeanor. Every time she phoned the investment company where her late husband had worked and failed to get through to the executive she sought, she seemed more and more anxious, not to mention frustrated.

It was late one afternoon of the second week before she was finally able to connect. Thad heard the relief in her voice. He also noted how happy she was to speak with the other man. The jolt of jealousy that shot through him was a real surprise.

Lindy's eyes brightened and a smile accompanied her greeting. "Mr. Reed! I'm so glad I finally reached you. This is Lindy Southerland."

Judging by her widening grin, the executive was receiving her call without reservations.

"Fine, thank you," Lindy said. "I hate to bother you but I need a small favor. You know that account where you've been sending my checks? I've had to close it."

Again she paused, glancing at Thad and nodding as she listened to Reed's reply.

"That's right. I won't be using that bank at all anymore. I'm moving my accounts to Arkansas and I was hoping you'd be able to hold any further payments until I can get you the new numbers for direct deposit."

She flashed Thad an okay signal that eased his mind a little.

"No, there's no problem you need to be concerned about. I just decided it was sensible to keep my money where I could access it more easily."

Thad had gotten to his feet and was about to leave the office when he heard her sharp intake of breath.

"Oh, dear."

He spun around. Mouthed, *What?*

Lindy merely shook her head and held up a hand to signal him to wait.

Continuing to listen, he saw her eyes grow misty.

"No. No, it's not your fault. You've been more than kind to Danny and me. I understand. Don't worry about us. We'll be fine." She sniffled slightly. "Thank you for everything, Mr. Reed."

Ending the call, Lindy looked to Thad. "He says it won't matter about my new bank account because he's already paid me for all of Ben's sick leave and overtime. There won't be any more checks coming."

"Then you'll have to keep working for me," Thad said, hoping his smile was genuine enough to encourage her. "See? It all worked out."

"Except for the house payments the bank claims I owe. Ben was making a lot of money when we bought that house. The monthly payments were exorbitant."

"One crisis at a time, okay?"

"Okay." To his relief, Lindy began to smile. "How are you coming with my messed-up computer records?"

"Still plugging away. In the meantime, it's a good thing you wrote that protest letter to the Georgia State Banking Department the way the woman on the phone suggested. I did a little research. Involving a lawyer doesn't do any good."

"I can't afford one anyway."

"I told you we'd work something out if you needed more help."

"And I told you I'd manage. Everything will work out."

Thad knew it was futile to argue. The fact that he had met and hired Lindy at just the right time struck him as possibly divine intervention. Beyond that, he figured they'd have to bide their time and wait to see what developed.

The more he pondered her situation, however, the more it seemed odd to him that her late husband's former boss would stop sending money at this precise time.

Sure, it might be nothing more than a coincidence but Thad's instincts made him wary.

He turned to Lindy. "Tell me. How well do you know this guy—the one who just told you he was going to stop your checks?"

"Mr. Reed? Well enough. He was very solicitous after Ben was killed. Why?"

"Something doesn't ring true, that's all. Doesn't it seem kind of odd to you that he would stop payments just when you were having other financial difficulties?"

"No. I didn't tell him I was."

"Suppose he already knew?"

"How would he? I haven't talked to anyone at the firm for months. It's my fault for not asking how long the checks were going to keep coming. I should have known they would stop someday. Ben never took sick time but that doesn't mean he'd accumulated an unlimited amount."

Thad shrugged. "Okay. If you say Reed's on the up-and-up, I'll accept your conclusion."

"Actually, he was the only one who even bothered to come up from Little Rock for Ben's funeral. It was as if the others he'd worked with were ashamed to show their faces. James was the one who helped me sort out Ben's papers after the authorities were through with them, too."

It was *James,* now? "Really? That is interesting."

He watched Lindy's face, saw her arch an eyebrow and press her lips into a thin line.

"Oh, no you don't," she said firmly. "Don't give me that suspicious look. I know what you're thinking and it's impossible. The feds did a thorough investigation of everyone who worked with Ben and nobody was in on the crime. He had been laundering money for drug smugglers through a hedge fund that he had set up and managed all by himself."

"What happened to that money after he died?" Thad asked.

"I assume the DEA got hold of it. Why?"

Thad drew his fingers down his cheek to the point of his chin, ending in a thoughtful pose. "I wonder. Suppose somebody thought you had it or knew where it was?"

"Then they know by now that I don't," Lindy countered. "I have no idea how large an amount was involved but I suspect it was a bundle. Believe me, if I had that kind of extra cash on hand, I wouldn't be worrying about credit cards and my meager savings account."

"I suppose you're right."

Lindy's smile blossomed. "Of course I am. I'm never wrong."

The effect of her grin warmed him to the core and he had to smile with her. "That claim may work with your little boy but I'm a lot older and wiser. I know you must have made at least one mistake sometime."

To his chagrin she immediately sobered and nodded before she said, "Yes. When I got married. Believe me, I am never going to try that again."

There was no good reason for Thad to argue with her, nor was he sure she was wrong about matrimony. His own parents had had a rotten marriage and if it hadn't been for seeing Rob and Ellen together, he might have thought wedded bliss was an impossible goal.

As it was, Thad knew better than to hope he could find a wife like Ellen. For one thing, he didn't deserve that kind of happiness.

For another, he wasn't able to be the kind of ideal husband his brother had been. Not even close.

Lindy fell into a comfortable daily routine. So did her son. And now that Danny knew Thad Pearson pretty well, she figured it was time she kept her promise to Samantha and took the boy to Sunday school.

They hadn't been back to Serenity Chapel since the day of Ben's funeral. At that time, Lindy had decided it would be easier to skip worship services than it would be to deal with the sidelong glances and the unspoken questions from members of the congregation.

Few church members had actually attended the short service that Brother Logan Malloy had conducted at her husband's graveside. Lindy's memories of that sad day were foggy but she recalled enough to feel pain. Abandonment. Loss.

Sometimes it was as if only a few days had passed since then. Other times, her life as a married woman seemed so remote that she saw those years as little more than a bad dream.

And now? Lindy asked herself. Now was now. She was finally making a stable home for Danny. Part of that newfound stability was directly due to her job and their relationship with Thad Pearson. If she was ever going to reintroduce her son to her faith, there might never be a better time.

Danny had pouted when she'd mentioned going to church again—until she'd told him who his Sunday school teacher would be. Then, he had beat her getting dressed and had even combed his unruly hair by himself.

She, too, was more excited than she'd expected to be. The dress she'd chosen was one that Ben had ridiculed simply because he didn't care for the color. Shades of purple were Lindy's favorite. And this outfit was one of the few she had picked out to please herself rather than her husband.

She didn't wish to analyze that choice too deeply. The dress had simply spoken to her. She'd loved it the moment she'd seen it in the shop and when she'd tried it on it had fit so perfectly she'd had to buy it.

Smoothing the slim skirt she sighed. Remembered. Almost cringed.

"Take that ugly thing off and put on something decent," Ben had shouted at her. He'd checked his watch. "And make it snappy. We're already running late."

Lindy recalled biting her lower lip to keep from weeping as she'd raced back to the bedroom to change. Ben favored dull colors that made her spirits flag. But she'd changed. For him. Because he was her husband and because she'd wanted to please him. It was just that the purple dress had made her feel so good.

And it still did, Lindy realized, smiling. Although there remained a niggling suspicion that her personal wardrobe choices were not all they should be, she intended to wear this dress. For herself.

And for Thad Pearson? she wondered silently.

Of course not.

Liar.

Am not.

Yes, you are.

Chuckling over having an argument with herself, Lindy picked up her purse, took her son's hand and led him to the car.

Today was going to be another big milestone in

their recovery. Today, Danny was going back to Sunday school.

And I'm going to face all those people who ignored Ben's funeral as if it wasn't worthy of their attendance.

Her chin jutted. Her spine stiffened. She could do this. She could walk into church with her head held high because...

Because Thad was going to be there, too. It was as simple as that.

Two men in business suits and dark glasses were waiting for Thad when he left his house. Since it was Sunday morning he thought for an instant that they were dressed that way for church. Seconds later, he recognized their stiff demeanor.

If he'd been armed, he would have closed his hand around the butt of his pistol. That was how menacing they seemed.

"Your name Pearson?" the graying, older man asked without smiling.

"Maybe. Why?"

The second suited visitor stepped to one side so that Thad had to turn his head to watch him. The tactic was textbook. Divide and conquer.

Wary, Thad backed up. "What's all this about?"

"Simmer down, Sergeant," the first man said. "We're all on the same side here."

"In case you haven't heard, I'm a civilian," Thad said flatly. "Either tell me what's going on or get out of my way. I'm late for church."

"That's what your country likes, an honest man with good morals. You do have those, don't you, Pearson?"

Thad had disliked these two from the moment he'd set eyes on them and his opinion wasn't changing. Rather than continue useless verbal sparring, he folded his arms across his chest, concentrated on the obvious spokesman and waited.

"It's like this," the man finally said. "You've been poking your nose into affairs that are none of your business. Our department has gone to a lot of trouble to set up a sting and you're interfering."

"What sting? What department do you represent?"

"That's irrelevant. All you need to know is to back off and stop trying to help the enemy."

"You guys are crazy. I'd never do anything to hurt my country."

"But you are assisting a suspect in a criminal investigation."

Thad's blood turned to ice water in his veins. There was only one person he was going out of his way to help. Lindy Southerland.

"Are you telling me that an innocent woman who never hurt a soul is being set up?"

"Look," the agent said soberly, "we know you've been doing some computer hacking of your own and you're getting in our way. All we ask is that you stand down."

"While you ruin someone who doesn't have a crooked bone in her body? Give me one good reason why I should cooperate."

"New information has come to light. And because the only way any of us will ever be sure that Ben Southerland's widow isn't hiding millions in dirty money is if we force her to act."

"Or what? Suppose she doesn't know anything about the funds you're looking for? What then? Do you plan to let her be thrown out into the street?"

"If that's what it takes, yes," he replied with an arch of a graying brow. "Look, Sergeant. We aren't asking you to lie or stop employing the woman. Actually, we want you to continue befriending her so we'll have somebody on the inside who can tell us when she makes her move."

"No."

"You're willing to risk being indicted as an accessory?"

"I can't be an accessory if there's no crime," Thad countered. "I will stake my life that Lindy Southerland is innocent."

The younger, crew-cut agent chuckled quietly

before muttering, "Suits us. We'll take you both down if we have to."

Frowning at his cohort and pointing to their dark sedan, the older man handed Thad a business card and said, "We'll be in touch."

Thad watched them drive out of sight before he studied the card. It told him basically nothing, not even which government agency the men represented, and he realized belatedly that he had not been shown any badge or official ID, either.

Slipping the card into his jacket pocket, he vowed to call the number later just to see who answered. If that didn't tell him anything helpful, he'd do whatever his conscience told him to do next.

Right now, it was telling him that his defense of Lindy and Danny was only beginning and if he didn't hurry, he wouldn't be there when they arrived at church.

Fortunately, he spotted them pulling into the lot mere moments after he'd parked. He jogged up to their car and opened the driver's door. "Good morning!"

"Morning."

"I'm glad I got here in time," Thad said as Lindy climbed out. "I was afraid you might change your mind if I wasn't around."

She smoothed her skirt. "I promised we'd be here. I always keep my promises."

"Good for you." Thad reached to ruffle the boy's hair and was surprised when Danny ducked out of reach.

"He got ready all by himself this morning. Even combed his hair. Doesn't he look nice?"

"Not half as great as his mother looks," Thad said, smiling and cupping her elbow to guide her into Serenity Chapel.

"You don't think this dress is too bright?"

"It's perfect. You've never looked prettier."

Trailing them, Danny gave a loud, "Ewww," making both adults chuckle.

Thad glanced over his shoulder with a smile. "Hush. It's not polite to contradict grown-ups, especially when somebody's saying something nice."

He opened the heavy glass door to the brick building and held it for them to pass.

An usher inside handed Lindy a bulletin and gave her a welcoming smile. "Good morning, folks."

"Morning, Bob," Thad said. "You remember Mrs. Southerland and Danny, don't you?"

"Sure do," the older man replied, his grin spreading. "Good to see you again, ma'am."

"Thank you."

"Danny is going to be in my class, so if you

catch him wandering around, just point him in the right direction."

As they walked down the hallway, Lindy looked up at Thad. "Why would Danny be wandering anywhere? If he's in your class I'll expect him to stay there."

"Unless he needs a bathroom break or wants a drink of water."

On cue, the boy broke away and ran to the water fountain.

"See what I mean? Most of the boys in my class are good kids but they are kids. When one suggests a drink, all of them want one. It's natural."

"I guess so. I just…"

"Would you like to come in with him? I don't mind."

"Is that wise?"

"If you want my honest opinion, no. Having his mama there, watching his every move, might be a bit stifling."

"You're right. I just hate to leave him."

Drawing a finger in an X across his chest, Thad raised his other hand as if taking a solemn oath. "I promise to keep an eye on him and deliver him to you in the sanctuary right after class. Sit in the back row so we can find you easily, okay?"

"Okay." Nodding, she sighed. "I'll hang around out here in the hall until I'm sure he's settled, then go into one of the women's classes. I don't want to go back into the couples' group Ben and I used to belong to."

"Fine." Thad held the classroom door for Danny, followed him through and began to introduce him to the other boys who had already arrived.

Glancing back as the door swung shut, he saw a flash of Lindy's purple dress and hoped she'd trust him enough to take his advice. There was a point at which she was going to make her child feel trapped if she wasn't careful. Parents walked a fine line between overprotectiveness and neglect.

The age and maturity of a child had a lot to do with their perception, of course. So did their peers. That was where being brought up in the church helped.

Anybody could go astray. What Thad tried to teach his class was how to own up to it and turn their lives around if they realized they were headed in the wrong direction.

A lot of adults could use that same lesson, he mused, hoping that his judgment of Lindy's innocence wasn't being skewed by his emotions.

Thad gritted his teeth. He could not be wrong about her. So why was she in the crosshairs of some obscure government agency and what was he going to do about it?

In retrospect, he wished he'd thought to ask the agents why they had resorted to breaking and entering and why they had left such a disgusting thing in her kitchen.

"If they did," he muttered.

Suddenly uneasy at the direction of his thoughts, he glanced toward the door, imagining the lovely woman he'd left in the hallway.

If they had been anywhere but in church, he would have been a lot more worried.

NINE

Standing outside the door alone hadn't bothered Lindy until the classes had started and the passing crowd thinned. There were still official greeters stationed at the exterior doors but other than them and a few late arrivals, she was all by herself.

She turned her back to the wall beside Danny's classroom and folded her arms. Her dress had long sleeves and the loose, uneven jacket hem fell below the belted waist, making the outfit well suited to early spring weather, so why was she shivering?

On the opposite side of the closed door, she could hear Thad beginning to lead the children in prayer. Reedy little voices added the names of others for whom they were praying before she heard her son.

"I wanna pray for my daddy," Danny said. "He died."

"Go ahead," Thad urged.

Holding her breath and straining to hear, Lindy

couldn't make out Danny's response. It had apparently been negative because the teacher then spoke for him.

"Father, we want to ask You to help our new friend, Danny, and his mother. You know what they need and we trust You to take good care of them. Please help Danny to understand why his daddy is gone and not be too sad. Amen."

A tear slid down Lindy's cheek. She pressed her fingertips to her lips, ducked her head and hurried to the nearby ladies' restroom.

Thankfully, it was deserted. She grabbed a handful of tissues and blotted her face before blowing her nose and peering at her image in the mirror above the sink.

Her mascara was smeared, her nose was red and her eyes were getting puffy. She couldn't enter a new class looking like that. It was too reminiscent of the way she had often appeared after one of Ben's tirades and she was certainly not going to give that impression again.

The only sensible option was to wait outside in her car for an hour or so until the main worship service began. That would give her enough time to pull herself together so she didn't look as if she was upset.

Concentrating on escape, Lindy rushed into the parking lot and keyed the remote control to unlock her car. She was about to toss her purse in ahead of her when she looked down at the black leather seat.

Another note!

Her first reaction was relief that it hadn't come attached to anything revolting or dead or both.

Then, she bent closer and peered at it.

It was in Ben's handwriting. Again. And it referred to money, which made sense since he'd made his living managing funds for lots of people. The question was, where had these old memos come from and who was leaving them for her?

An additional jolt of adrenaline suddenly brought her to full awareness. This wasn't simply another foray into her home. It was far worse.

Someone had followed her to church. Had broken into her car without leaving any sign of tampering.

Not only was that frightening, it was a sure sign that she was still being watched. Perhaps, even at that moment, her enemies were closing in.

There was only one smart thing to do. One place to go that was safe.

Lindy slammed the car door, ran back into the chapel past the surprised-looking greeter and made a beeline straight for Thad Pearson's classroom.

Her hand was reaching for the knob when she came to her senses and paused. If she burst into that room, her son was going to be mortified, everybody was going to get upset and she was liable to scare those poor kids silly—not to mention their teacher.

Although she was trembling, inside and out, Lindy pulled herself together enough to reason. She needed to call the sheriff herself, meet them in the parking lot when they arrived and calmly make the report.

Until a few weeks ago she wouldn't have had anyone to turn to. No family. No close friends except maybe Samantha. And definitely no Thad Pearson. Therefore, what she needed to do was act the part of the strong, self-reliant woman she kept insisting she was.

"I am," Lindy assured herself. "I don't need babysitting, I don't need a man and I don't need…"

She slowly backed away from the door to Danny's class while feeling around in her shoulder bag for her cell phone. She'd been about to voice the troubling thought that she didn't even need divine help—and do so while standing inside a church, of all places!

Flipping open her phone she hesitated and murmured, "Sorry, Father. I know better than that. I'm just so…"

What? Scared? Confused? Alone?

The first two, maybe. The last, no. She might be standing in an empty hallway and shaking like a leaf in a gale but she wasn't alone. She never had been. It wasn't that the Lord had forsaken her. She had turned her back on *Him*.

Yet, in spite of her actions and her hardened heart, God had sent a warrior, a defender, into her life.

Mere feet away, on the other side of that classroom door, was Thad Pearson. He guarded her son better than she ever could.

She might manage to convince herself that the cyber attacks on her finances were random but she would never believe for a second that meeting Thad and making such an easy connection with him had not been divinely inspired.

Thankful beyond words, Lindy whispered, "Thank You, Jesus," lifted the phone and called the sheriff.

Flashing red lights were the first thing Thad noticed through the church's side windows when he dismissed his class and headed toward the sanctuary with Danny.

The boy tugged on his hand and pointed. "Look! That's my mama."

"I see her."

"C'mon. Let's go."

"Hold your horses," Thad said. "She looks fine. We don't want to distract her while she's busy with the policeman."

He scooped up Danny and carried him rather

than take a chance the child would take off and run across the lot. Some worshippers were just arriving for the main service while a few others were leaving. The last thing Lindy needed was to have her son carelessly racing through traffic.

The boy looped an arm around Thad's neck. His obvious trust and reliance touched the ex-marine and carried his thoughts back to other children in other countries. Children he had tried to help in spite of orders to keep his distance.

Lindy seemed to sense their approach. She turned and waved. "Hi, guys."

"What happened?" Thad asked evenly. He wanted to shout at her, to chastise her for coming outside without him, but he figured that wasn't such a good idea, especially in view of the negative reaction she'd had to his nightmare.

"I found another note. In the car. On the seat," Lindy said. "I called to report it, expecting the sheriff to respond. The church is in the city so I got the police, instead." She gave a weak smile. "You know Samantha's husband, John, don't you?"

"Yes." Thad paused long enough to offer to shake the man's hand before he said, "What I don't understand is why you were out here in the first place. You weren't planning to ditch me and my little buddy, were you?" He felt the child's grip tighten.

"Of course not. I planned to meet you for church, just like I promised."

"So, John, are you done with Lindy?" Thad asked the solemn-looking officer.

"Apparently."

"What about the note? Did you pick it up already?"

"No. We didn't find anything. I guess she was mistaken."

Thad frowned, first at John Waltham, then at Lindy.

She shrugged. "I know I didn't imagine it. There was a note lying right there on the seat. It looked like the one we found at my house, only it was just loose paper. And definitely Ben's handwriting."

"You searched the entire car?" Thad asked.

"Yes," Lindy replied, cocking her head in the direction of the waiting officer. "First John did, then I did, after he said he couldn't find any sign of it."

"And it was really gone."

"Unfortunately."

Thad saw Lindy shiver so he stepped closer and slipped his free arm around her waist. "Okay. Since all the excitement is over, let's go back inside and warm up." He eyed the other man. "Thanks."

"Any time. If you see my wife inside, tell her I have another call so I can't join her this morning."

The black-and-white was driving away when Lindy asked Thad, "You do believe me, don't you?"

"Oh, yeah. I believe you. I also know that who-ever left the note in the first place, then got rid of it before the cops came, had to be watching you. That's why I didn't want to stand around in the parking lot where we were too exposed."

"I'd thought of that, too. I figured as long as there was a police car right there I'd be safe enough."

"You were only safe assuming Waltham was as alert as he should have been. I got the idea his mind was on wanting to join his wife in church, more than it was on his job."

"I think it's nice that guys like John get to go to services while they're on duty, but I really wish I hadn't called anyone this time," Lindy said. "You should have seen the looks I got when I had to stand out there by the police car and talk to him. People already suspected I might be a crook be-cause of Ben. Now, they're going to be sure I am."

"They just need to get to know you the way I do." *And I will never believe you're anything but totally honest, no matter how many spooks in black suits and sunglasses try to convince me otherwise.*

"Has it occurred to you that it might be best if I moved away? Left Serenity?" she asked softly.

The idea of Lindy purposely stepping out of his life hit Thad like a sucker punch. He could not let her do that. Not now. Maybe not ever.

Because I need to be nearby to protect her, he insisted silently.

That much was true. The problem was, there was a lot more to his motives than simply guarding Lindy and her son. The mere thought of not having her involved in his life cut to the quick. She was his God-given assignment, among other things, and he was not about to shirk that duty.

You care too much already, his conscience insisted.

Thad had no rebuttal for such raw truth. He did care. For Lindy and for Danny. It was as if he'd been given a chance to atone for not only his actions in combat but also for his failure to avert the tragedy that had taken his brother's life.

That rationale made little sense, yet Thad clung to it with a desperation that came straight from his core.

As Lindy entered the sanctuary with Thad and her son, she was almost overcome by her emotions again.

Being that disturbed, that moved, came as a shock to her. She'd had no idea how much she'd truly missed coming here or how deep her feelings for this particular body of believers went. Her late husband had always been the one to insist they attend—looking for business contacts—

and until this very moment Lindy had not realized how much this pastor and congregation had meant to her, personally.

Although she had assumed she was angry to have been ignored, what she was really feeling was a terrible loss of belonging, of being a part of God's family.

Now, standing in the rear of the sanctuary, she could finally see that a lot of her isolation came from her own choices. *She* had decided to stop coming to church. *She* had failed to return calls from the few people who had reached out to her. And *she* had refused to agree when Pastor Malloy had suggested counseling.

Walking beside her, Thad leaned closer to ask, "Front or back?"

"Definitely the back, if you think we're not too late," Lindy whispered. "Remember that old joke? You have to come to church early to find a seat in the rear."

"I know."

Eyes downcast, she joined him in the closest pew, thankful he'd managed to find room for them without leading her all the way to the front past so many curious worshippers.

It was embarrassing to have admitted how standoffish and unfriendly she'd been and she was still coming to terms with her confusion over where the real blame lay. Some of it was undoubtedly hers, yet she kept wondering if there wasn't some way to pass it off on others.

That silly thought amused her. It also hit her in her conscience. If there was ever a perfect place to admit to a failing and find peace, it was right here.

Danny cuddled up to her as soon as Thad put him down and she smiled at the boy. "Can you sit nice and still for Mama?"

"Uh-huh."

As Lindy watched, the child looped one arm through her elbow and the other through Thad's. He had never acted that way with his father. Never.

I am not going to cry again, she insisted. *I am not.*

Still, unshed tears gathered and dampened her lashes. Fighting to temper her emotions, she couldn't even give thanks in prayer because she knew that doing so would release a flood of weeping and embarrass everyone, especially Thad.

But she was overwhelmingly thankful—and sure that the Lord knew what lay in her deepest heart. The world outside these walls might be against her but, in here, she had found true sanctuary. Real peace.

Lindy chanced a sidelong glance at Thad, saw how lovingly he was looking at Danny, and added one more element to her burgeoning gratitude. Thad Pearson.

* * *

During the service, Thad had to keep forcing his attention back to Logan Malloy's sermon. That took monumental effort because what he wanted to do was mull over his early morning encounter with the government agents and try to figure out his next move.

If he broke silence and confided everything to Lindy she might inadvertently do something that made her look guilty when she wasn't. However, if he left her in the dark and allowed her to muddle through the financial mess "big brother" had evidently dumped on her, she'd worry needlessly.

But she'd be safer from unwarranted prosecution that way, he argued. He had seen how upset she became if she thought she was about to be physically assaulted and had to assume that awareness of who was behind the financial attack would unhinge her.

This unnecessary harassment couldn't go on much longer. Lindy was already flat broke and her house was in foreclosure. If anyone was expecting her to access secret bank accounts to bail herself out, surely they'd soon see that she wasn't hiding anything like that.

Thad's thoughts drifted to James Reed, the executive who had recently informed Lindy that the checks from his firm were stopping. *Could he be in on it?* Possibly. Stranger things had happened. Especially lately.

When the congregation stood for the closing prayer, Thad was chagrined to realize he'd missed the second half of the sermon thanks to his musings.

Smiling at Lindy as they were dismissed and started walking out, he asked, "How about letting me treat you both to Sunday dinner?"

"That really isn't necessary," she said, "but thanks for asking."

"Aw, mama…."

"Danny wants to go eat, don't you, pal?"

"I want ice cream," the boy piped up.

"And I do owe you that since I totally forgot to bring any when we had spaghetti at your house."

"I put the leftover sauce in the freezer," Lindy said flatly. "We can go home and eat that."

Thad totally understood her rationale. Throwing away food was bad enough when a person had plenty of money. For a single mother struggling to feed her family it was unthinkable.

"Okay. Tell you what. I'll stop by the market and pick up some ice cream for dessert and maybe some garlic bread. Unless you want to come with me."

"I don't expect you to spend every moment looking after us," Lindy countered. "We'll be just fine." She began to grin. "Though, yes, you're welcome to join us if you really want to."

Talk about embarrassing. He had just invited himself to her house for another meal and hadn't even realized he was doing it. Thinking back on her exact words, she hadn't mentioned including him in their Sunday dinner, he had simply assumed that was her intent.

Lindy's genial laugh helped relieve some of his discomfiture. Maybe she had meant for him to be included all along and had been teasing. He sure hoped so.

Returning her grin, Thad knew his cheeks were flushed because he could feel the creeping warmth. When his gaze met hers and he saw the twinkle in her emerald eyes he was positive he'd been the target of a subtle joke.

"Sorry," Lindy said, still chuckling. "I couldn't resist. Just go get the ice cream. We'll meet you back at the house."

He reached for her, gently touched her arm through her sleeve. "Come with me to the store?"

"Why?"

"I don't know. Call it a hunch if you want. I'd just feel better if we stuck pretty close after—" he glanced at her car "—you know."

"I'm not going to let some sicko run my life," Lindy insisted. "I'll go home and defrost the spaghetti sauce while you shop. I was careful to lock all the new dead bolts you installed. Nobody strange will be in the house."

How could he argue with such a sensible plan? "Okay, you win. My truck is right over there. I'll wait 'til I see you're on your way and then head for the market."

Traffic around them was already thinning as other worshippers filed out of the lot in a slow convoy of cars and trucks. Until churches dismissed on Sunday mornings, the streets of Serenity were virtually deserted—except for the flatlanders— the tourists—who happened to be passing through town on their way to recreational areas. Right after twelve noon, long lines formed at all the local restaurants. If a preacher talked longer than usual, his followers generally had to wait quite a while to eat unless they, too, opted to dine at home.

Thad climbed into his truck and watched Lindy drive away slowly, cautiously, smiling and politely waving to give others permission to pull out in front of her.

There was no way a sweet woman like that was knowingly hiding a stash of loot from her late husband's criminal activities. It simply wasn't possible. Lindy was kind. Honest. Forthright. There wasn't a crooked bone in her body. All a person had to do was look at her to see how totally innocent she was.

Like the women who strapped bombs to their

bodies, or worse, to their children, and pretended to be victims, themselves? Thad's conscience asked with a kick to his stomach and a prickling of the short hairs on the nape of his neck.

He had experienced that kind of cruel subterfuge while serving overseas and had fallen victim to it once. He had chosen to befriend the wrong pitiful-looking, street urchin and some of his friends had paid for his error in judgment by being seriously wounded.

Guilt over that terrible mistake still haunted him. Worse, he knew that the military shrinks who had forced him to retire had been right. He had lost the vital ability to reason rationally during a battle and had no longer been a leader his comrades-in-arms could count on.

Thad knew that stepping aside had been the right decision. For the good of the corps.

His main concern was whether his overall judgment could still be trusted—particularly where Lindy Southerland was concerned. He sure hoped so.

TEN

The strange sedan waiting on one side of Lindy's wide driveway when she got home gave her the willies. Who was it? And why were they just sitting there?

She had almost convinced herself to put her car in Reverse and flee when a tall, distinguished-looking gentleman with a thick head of graying-black hair climbed out of the parked vehicle. He straightened his suit coat and tie before raising a hand to wave.

Recognition dawned. Lindy began to grin. Parking parallel to the other car, she helped Danny undo his seat belt, then greeted their visitor.

"Mr. Reed! What a nice surprise. What brings you to Serenity?"

He took her hand when she offered it but instead of merely shaking it he clasped it firmly. "Hello, Lindy. Danny. I was worried after you called the other day. How are you doing?"

"We're okay," she said, sobering. "I have had

some financial reverses recently but it's all a big mistake. My boss is helping me sort things out."

"So, you do have a job?"

"Yes. I'm an executive assistant at Pearson Products, right here in Serenity."

"Never heard of them. What do they handle?"

"Kitchen gadgets, mostly," Lindy said.

"How...interesting."

"I think it is," she said, noting with disappointment how quickly the man's attitude had become dismissive.

Now what? Lindy wondered. The polite thing to do was to invite him to join them for Sunday dinner. That wouldn't have caused any consternation if Thad had not been expected, too. She didn't want to expose her friend to the kind of snobbery she'd just glimpsed if she could help it. Still, what real choice did she have?

"We were planning to have a simple spaghetti dinner in about an hour. If you can stay..."

"Love to," Reed said. "I've been wanting to check in on you and see for myself that you're all right. I apologize for not doing so sooner."

"There's really no need for you to feel responsible."

"Nonsense. Ben was one of our most valued employees until that unfortunate incident with the hedge fund." He leaned closer to speak as he followed Lindy toward the house. "I never did think he was as involved as the authorities claimed. And if he was, he must have had good reasons for the decisions that led to such a tragic end."

"Really?" Lindy was flabbergasted. Ben had been as guilty as sin and everyone knew it, from the local police all the way up to the top agents in the DEA. His private papers and computer files had proved it beyond a doubt.

Yet, here stood one of the men whose firm had borne the brunt of the bad publicity and he was defending Ben's morals. Could he be that clueless? That forgiving?

Or was he simply trying to get on her good side by praising her late husband? If the latter was true, he clearly didn't know what kind of man Ben had been in his private life.

It took Lindy a few extra seconds to unlock the door and let them all in because of the additional dead bolt Thad had installed.

"You seem to be secure enough," Reed commented as she led the way inside.

"We've had several break-ins recently. The heavier locks were necessary."

"I thought this was a peaceful little town."

"It was. It is," Lindy countered. "Most of the time, anyway."

"What in the world could burglars be after? I mean, you don't keep a lot of cash lying around, do you?"

That ridiculous question made her chuckle. "Not hardly. Until I found my new job, I was relying on the monthly checks you were sending."

"You're quite welcome. I was glad to be able to help."

Wandering through the kitchen and into the main part of the first floor ahead of her, Reed showed an interest in the home that surprised Lindy.

Danny had not warmed to him, however, and was keeping his distance. Given the boy's fondness for Thad, the contrast was glaring.

"You don't have much in here worth selling if you need to raise money." Reed spoke from the doorway to the living room. "No art or expensive collectibles."

"I'll manage." Lindy was beginning to lose patience with the man. If he had not previously intervened on her behalf and arranged to send her Ben's unpaid sick leave, she might have been tempted to snap at him for such derogatory comments. True or not.

"I might be able to come up with something like a finder's fee if you and I were able to track down any accounts your husband didn't choose to report."

"What?"

Lindy had been occupied removing the plastic

container of sauce from the freezer and wasn't sure she'd heard correctly.

"I said, you might be due a finder's fee."

"For what? Nothing is lost." Her brow knit. "Is it?"

Reed shrugged the well-padded shoulders of his silk suit and regarded her seriously. "One never knows. Anything is possible in this age of computer transfers and offshore accounts."

Rejoining her in the kitchen as she set the microwave to defrost the Italian sauce, he seemed to be trying to peer inside her mind, making Lindy feel like a bug under a microscope.

She whirled to face him. "I don't have a clue what you're talking about. Should I?"

Another shrug was accompanied by a slight smile. "Perhaps, if you think hard enough, something will come to mind."

Lindy busied herself drawing water for a fresh batch of pasta while she tried to sort through her confusion. James Reed clearly believed, as had other outsiders, that Ben had kept money in secret accounts. Maybe it was true—she didn't know. She had never been privy to her husband's business decisions. Ben had not only excluded her from his day-to-day dealings, he had inferred that she was too stupid to have understood the details even if he had chosen to explain them.

"Look, Mr. Reed..."

"James. Please?"

"All right, James. I really have no idea if there are accounts out there that Ben kept hidden. If there are, he certainly never confided in me. I know some men may choose to tell their wives about the deals they make but my husband was not like that. Looking back, I have to assume he kept it all to himself, especially during the last few years of his life, because he knew I would never condone anything dishonest or illegal."

"Of course not. I certainly didn't mean to imply otherwise."

Lindy was about to assure him that she wasn't upset when the back door opened.

Thad shouldered through with grocery sacks in his arms and demanded, "Whose car is that?"

She swept an arm toward her first guest. "This is Mr. Reed, from Little Rock. He's the one I phoned from your office a couple days ago. Remember? Thad Pearson, James Reed."

Thad dropped the plastic grocery bags onto the countertop and extended his hand. "A pleasure."

Watching the faces of both men, Lindy was a little amused. They were eyeing each other like two bulldogs meeting unexpectedly in disputed territory. Thad was smiling—sort of—and offering to shake hands, while James was acting as if he couldn't decide whether or not to accept the friendly gesture.

Finally, they joined hands and shook, forcefully yet briefly.

Oh, my, Lindy thought, turning away and stifling a smirk. This was really going to be an interesting afternoon. She just hoped her guests didn't come to blows before it was over.

To say that Thad had been surprised to find anyone else in Lindy's kitchen was an understatement. He'd been floored.

The well-dressed executive seemed totally out of place there in spite of his history with the same investment firm where Ben Southerland had worked. This guy Reed was too slick. Too neat. And acting way too friendly and solicitous around Lindy to suit Thad.

She had prepared the formal dining room table, too, making Thad suspect she was either putting on airs for the benefit of her other guest or extending him preferential treatment because his opinion mattered to her. Neither notion sat well.

Danny had appeared and begun acting pretty normal as soon as he'd spotted Thad. That was a good sign. The way they had been seated at the table, however, was not.

Lindy and Reed were on one side of the modern, oblong table while Danny had latched onto Thad and insisted he sit next to him.

That arrangement gave Thad a direct view of

both Lindy and her other guest. It was not pleasing to see them shoulder to shoulder. And, unless he missed his guess, Reed had scooted his chair closer to hers as soon as he'd politely seated her. Not only that, he was countering the moves she seemed to be making in reaction to increase her distance from him.

"Oops. I forgot the garlic bread Thad brought," Lindy said, jumping up and dropping her napkin beside her plate. "I'll be right back."

Reed and Thad both stood.

"I can get it for you," Thad said.

"No, no. I'm the hostess. I'll do it."

He muttered, "You might burn yourself on the oven," as he trailed her into the kitchen, trying to keep from stomping his feet.

Her eyes were wide, innocent, when she looked back at him. "Really. I can handle it."

"Can you handle *him?*" Thad whispered, cocking his head toward the dining room. "That guy is as oily as they come."

"I don't know what you mean."

"Why did he come here? What does he want? If there's no more money to give you, why show up on your doorstep at all?"

"He's just trying to be helpful," Lindy explained. "He says, if we can find any accounts that Ben may not have reported, I can get a nice reward."

"We? As in you and Mr. Oily?"

"James is simply a polished businessman. I admit he doesn't fit in Serenity but neither did Ben. Not really. He was too stuffy."

Thad took the padded mitt from her and bent to open the oven door. "Is that the kind of man you like?" he asked, lifting the baking sheet and setting it on the top of the stove next to the pasta pot.

Instead of replying, Lindy scowled at him.

"Hey, forget it," Thad added. "It's none of my business who you hang around with. I'm just telling you to be careful, that's all."

"Careful of what?"

Of looking guilty. Of getting involved with another crook or wheeler-dealer. He couldn't come right out and say that, of course. Not without first calling the number on the business card the senior agent had handed him that morning and getting permission.

Thad wondered if those investigators would be interested in learning about Reed's visit and the suggestions he'd made to Lindy.

Unless they're the ones who sent him, Thad reasoned, growing even more suspicious. If Reed was working with the others, it was possible that he'd been asked to try to get Lindy to reveal secrets that Ben had taken with him to the grave. That was actually a more plausible conclusion than the idea that the man was acting on his own.

Then again, if Reed was being less than honest with Lindy, there was a chance he was after ill-gotten gains, himself. Since he had been Ben's superior, it was possible he'd been aware of far more than he'd admitted.

Watching Lindy place the hot bread in a basket and cover it with a linen cloth, Thad had to stop himself from taking her arm, from forcing her to look him in the eye so he could better judge her true feelings.

If he restrained her, even slightly, would she react positively or recoil the way she had when he'd awakened from his nightmare flashback?

He wasn't going to find out because he wasn't going to touch her. Period. There would be plenty of time for private conversations when they were at work. In the meantime, he planned to keep his distance and silently observe—unless this guy in the expensive suit and silk tie stepped out of line.

Thad almost smiled at the thought of literally defending Lindy against someone he clearly saw as a villain.

She'd never buy that conclusion, of course. He knew she wouldn't. But that didn't keep him from wishing he could bodily toss the slick interloper out the door. And out of her life.

As the afternoon wore on into evening and neither of her guests gave any indication of being the first to leave, Lindy wondered what she was going to do.

Danny had fallen asleep on the couch. When Thad offered to carry him upstairs and put him to bed, she hoped that would break the stalemate.

Alone with James Reed, she was surprised when he crossed to her and clasped her hand, cradling it in both of his.

"You need to give my suggestion some serious thought, Lindy," he said quietly.

She noticed that although he was speaking to her, his attention kept diverting toward the stairway leading to the second floor. It didn't take a trained psychologist to see that he was watching for Thad's return.

"I know you're just trying to help me," she replied. "But I'm afraid it's hopeless. If Ben did have hidden accounts, I have no idea where to look for them. Surely, you must be in a better position to do that than I am."

"Not really." Reed shook his head and set his jaw. "We did find a few indications of other activity on Ben's office computer but nothing definitive."

"Then maybe there was nothing to find."

"Possibly not. He did do a lot of work from home, though."

"The authorities confiscated the personal computer that was in his office upstairs. If there was anything odd on it, I'm sure their techs would have discovered it by now."

"I suppose so. Still…"

"All right. I promise I'll try to recall anything Ben may have mentioned and let you know if I do."

"It's not for me, it's for you," he insisted. "There will be a generous reward if we're able to turn more laundered funds over to the powers that be. And your country will be grateful."

Patriotism, too? She almost laughed. The man was pulling out all the stops.

Footsteps thudded on the stairs behind her. Lindy pulled free of Reed's grasp, slightly embarrassed to have allowed him to hold her hand that way.

Although she would have liked Thad to stay a little longer she figured the only way she was going to get any peace that evening was to suggest that both men leave.

"James was just saying good-night," Lindy announced brightly. A theatrical yawn punctuated her statement. "I'm sorry to see you gentlemen go, but I'm really exhausted. I hope you don't mind."

"I'll have to move my truck so he can get out anyway," Thad said. "I blocked him in when I got here."

She hoped she looked suitably contrite as she caught his eye and mouthed *Sorry.*

That would have been fine if James Reed had not taken her hand again and pulled her close enough to place a brief kiss on her cheek as he bid her goodbye.

The expression on Thad's handsome face was hard to read. It initially seemed to reflect anger, jealousy. Then sadness took over and he turned away.

That final mood was the one that touched Lindy's heart and made her want to reach out to him. To wrap her arms around him the way she had when they'd had their emotionally charged encounter in the yard. To lay her cheek on his chest where she could hear the hammering of his heart melding with her own.

"I'll see you tomorrow," she called after him.

The door slammed.

James Reed also took his leave after loitering another few minutes and babbling about how he had her best interests at heart.

Finally, Lindy was alone. Twisting the dead bolt, she leaned her forehead against the door and closed her eyes.

"Lord, what's going on?" she prayed in a soft whisper. "Tell me? Please? I'm so confused."

A few elements of her conundrum were clear. One man had been generous in the past but he now wanted something she could not provide.

The other man, Thad Pearson, wanted to give,

not take. He had been nothing but helpful and supportive. Yet the single thing she was beginning to want from him, he had insisted was beyond reach. She wanted his heart.

Pausing beside Reed's luxury sedan, Thad waited, almost wishing he'd have to go back inside and literally throw the guy out.

Oh, that would please Lindy, he grumbled to himself. She'd clearly been taken in by the man's polished exterior even if Danny hadn't.

As Reed made his way off the porch, Thad observed him closely. Some of the swagger was gone from his step and he looked as if his shoulders were sagging slightly. That was as much of a surprise as finding him there in the first place had been.

"You ready to go?" Thad called.

"As soon as you move your truck."

The way the man's graying eyebrow arched when he spoke gave Thad the notion that his old pickup had not made a favorable impression.

"We need to talk, first."

"Oh? I don't see why."

Thad was not deterred. "Who sent you?"

"I have no idea what you mean." Although he tried to edge close enough to open his car door, Thad remained in his way. "Excuse me?"

"Not until you level with me. It was those guys from the DEA or wherever, wasn't it?"

Reed scowled. "Who?"

"The spooks. They caught me this morning on my way to church and they were asking the same kinds of questions you kept asking Lindy."

"I don't know what you're talking about. Please move your vehicle. I have a long drive ahead of me."

Thad did step back but he remained unconvinced. "Okay. Suit yourself. But I'm telling you the same thing I told them. There is no way that woman is guilty of anything even a little bit shady. If you knew her the way I do, you'd see that."

The narrowing of the man's brows gave his eyes a menacing look. "You don't say."

"I do say."

"I'd be careful if I were you, Pearson. When and if Ms. Southerland's actions in this regard are exposed, you may find yourself on the wrong side of the law, too."

Astounded, Thad watched Reed climb behind the wheel and start his car. Ever since they had met that afternoon, Thad had been assuming the man was merely a shyster. Now, however, it looked as if he was working with whoever had set up the sting against Lindy.

That made sense. By cutting off the checks she'd been living on, they had hoped to force her to access Ben's phantom accounts. Reed was a part of that plan. Therefore, his visit today probably was, too.

Would it help to warn her? Thad wondered.

He didn't know how to do that without making things worse. If he told her of his suspicions against James Reed, he'd have to also explain who he believed the man was working with.

His one call to the number on the plain business card the supposed government agents had handed him had proved useless. The unlisted number was answered by a machine that gave no indication which agency was involved or who the men's superiors might be. For all Thad knew, those two guys might be acting on their own, or at least be part of a rogue outfit that officially answered to no one.

He had seen enough covert action himself to know how easily that kind of mission could be arranged. Often, the actual faces of the agency were so irrelevant that anyone could take their place. If that was the case this time, it didn't matter who had delivered the threats about Lindy's involvement. What was important was who had decided she held crucial secrets.

Backing into the street and letting his motor idle, Thad prepared to trail Reed all the way out of town before going home, himself. At this point he didn't care whether or not anyone was suspicious of his actions. Reed had already made enough threats to have scared off most self-appointed guardians.

That tactic wasn't going to work with Thad. He knew his duty and he knew his friends.

Lindy was innocent.

Nobody was going to change his mind about that.

ELEVEN

Lindy had been afraid that Thad would act aloof in the ensuing days and weeks because of having had to share that Sunday dinner with her surprise guest. To her relief, he not only seemed to have put the whole incident out of his mind, he was behaving as if she was just another employee. That might have pleased her if she hadn't begun visualizing herself as perhaps having a bigger place in his life someday.

Thankfully, their working relationship continued on an even keel. She was making a big dent in the backlog of paperwork for the company and Danny had settled in to a regular, after-school routine.

Lindy had tried to accept her daily challenges and carry on with as much tranquility as her son displayed in spite of ongoing confusion about her personal finances. The bank in Atlanta had turned her mortgage over to a collection agency but did acknowledge her formal complaint to the State

Banking Department. At least that was a step in the right direction. So was her new checking account and debit card at a local bank.

She checked the clock on the office wall, saw how late it was and smiled at her son. "Come on, Danny. Time to go home."

"Aww, Mom. Do we have to?"

"Yes, we have to."

Out of the corner of her eye, she saw Thad log off his computer, stand and stretch. She had long ago stopped asking if he'd had any more luck tracking down the glitches in her debt history. If he found anything, she knew he'd announce it loudly enough for the whole warehouse staff to overhear.

She chanced a smile because her mood insisted upon it and called good-night as she put on her coat.

"See you Sunday morning?" Thad replied.

It surprised her a little to realize it was already Friday. Another full week had passed. As they say, *How time flies when you're having fun.*

"Sure." Lindy gave him a little parting wave, grabbed her purse and shepherded her son out to the car.

Too bad Ben didn't hide any money the way Mr. Reed had suggested, she mused, wishing Pearson Products paid wages weekly instead of only twice a month. She could have put a hefty finder's fee to good use. *Oh, yeah.* Especially lately.

The heavy metal warehouse door banged and she looked up, knowing who else she would see leaving. Thad was still following her home each evening after work. Not that she minded. The detour wasn't a long one for him and his presence did give her a sense of safety that usually vanished as soon as he drove away.

He was still behind her when she turned off the highway onto Pilot Hill Drive—Snob Hill, in local parlance, because of its upscale housing. Several large trucks were parked in the vicinity of her address. That was odd.

Once she got closer she could see a gang of men. On her lawn! They were all wearing matching blue coveralls and either pushing dollies or carrying cardboard boxes to add to the stacks already piled outside the house.

Astounded, Lindy whipped into her driveway and jumped from the car, waving her arms and screaming, "Stop that. Put my things back!"

The crew toting belongings out of her house and placing them on the front lawn never missed a step.

Off to one side she spotted a patrol car. The sheriff was here, too. *Thank goodness!* Harlan could straighten all this out before it went any further.

Lindy was about to go appeal to him when another uniformed official approached and identified himself as a U.S. Marshal.

He touched the brim of his cap. "Mrs. Lindy Southerland?"

"Yes."

He handed her folded papers. Her hands were trembling as she opened and read the notarized eviction order.

"I'm sorry, ma'am," the marshal said. "This is always hard on everybody but it's the law."

"I don't understand. I thought we were getting this misunderstanding ironed out. I don't owe *anything* on my house. It's paid for."

"Not according to the collection agency," he said. "If there really is a mistake, you'll have to get a court order to that effect. There's nothing I can do tonight." He backed away. "I really am sorry."

Joining her, Thad took Danny's hand and said, "Don't panic. I'll bring the biggest box truck we have at work and ask a couple men from church to give us a hand loading your stuff so it's not left outside all night."

"No! This is wrong. They can't do this to me."

"Let me see that paperwork."

Lindy handed him the notice and watched him scan it before shaking his head. "I'm afraid they can. Roll with it, Lindy. We'll find a place for the two of you to stay temporarily."

Eyes wide and tear filled, she gaped at him.

How could he be so blasé? This was her home, her anchor. Her refuge. And she was being tossed out into the street because some computer hacker thought it would be funny to ruin her life? The whole thing was totally bizarre.

A couple salient points struck her. First, wasn't the collection agency supposed to contact her in person before taking such dire action? They had the office phone number and there had been no notification there. Second, if they had called her at home or sent registered letters, why had she not received them? Something definitely rotten was going on.

Leaving Thad to mind Danny, Lindy stomped across the grass to confront the sheriff. As far as she was concerned, this situation couldn't get more deplorable. There she was, out in the cold— literally—with all her possessions dumped on the lawn in plain sight of her neighbors and her boss. The only thing worse would be rain.

She glanced at the sky. No storm clouds marred the deepening blue of the evening while a few wisps of white on the western horizon gave color and texture to the pending sunset. So far, so good.

Angry at no one in particular because she didn't know who was interfering in her life, she had to really struggle to keep from taking her ire out on others. She knew Thad had been trying his best to help and that the marshal was just doing his job. She simply didn't understand why all this was happening to her.

"Sheriff," Lindy began as she neared the patrol car.

He held up a hand as if he were a traffic cop. The grimness of his expression silenced her. Behind him, she could see other deputies, including Adelaide Crowe, placing plastic bags into an open box that sat in the car's trunk.

"Lindy Southerland," the sheriff said flatly, "you're under arrest for possession of illegal substances. You have the right to remain silent..."

"No!"

As he droned on, Lindy wondered if she was going to suddenly awaken in her own bed and discover she'd been trapped in a terrible dream.

"You have the right to an attorney..."

The air thinned until Lindy could barely draw a usable breath. Her head was spinning. Her vision dimmed. Flashes of brightly colored light encroached. The earth tilted. Harlan's voice faded.

The last thing she remembered was hearing him shout, "Get her!" and wondering absently if she had somehow managed to escape the nightmare.

Drawn by the panic he heard in Lindy's raised voice, Thad arrived just in time to catch her as she fainted.

His gaze darted to Harlan. "What happened?"

"You'll need to let go of her, son. I'm afraid Miz Southerland is under arrest."

"That's ridiculous." Lifting Lindy in his arms, he took a step back. "She had every right to be upset about this travesty of justice. You can't arrest her for complaining."

The portly sheriff shook his head and Thad could see his distress. He didn't understand fully until Harlan said, "She's not being arrested for civil disobedience. We found a stash of drugs in her house."

"What? That's ridiculous. Lindy would never..."

"Doesn't matter," the sheriff argued. "The law's the law. I have to take her in."

"Why are you here in the first place?" Thad demanded.

"We got a tip."

"Oh, you did, did you?" Still cradling Lindy, he noticed that she was beginning to stir and mumble as she wrapped an arm around his neck.

Right then, in front of the sheriff and dozens of her neighbors, Thad wanted to kiss her the rest of the way to consciousness and assure her that everything would be okay. Except it wasn't okay. Not even close. And he had no idea what to do to make it so.

Scanning the yard, Thad saw Danny poking through a box of toys that had probably been taken from his room. Poor kid. He might not understand what was going on yet but he'd soon be devastated.

Before Harlan had a chance to decide what would become of the seven-year-old while his mother was in jail, Thad spoke up. "I've already arranged for Danny to spend the weekend with me so you won't have to worry about him."

"That so?"

"Yes. That's so." Thad knew he was doing the right thing for the child, he just wished he could do more for the mother.

Lindy was beginning to regain her faculties so he pulled her closer and bent to whisper in her ear. "I'll look after Danny. And I'll call a lawyer for you. I promise."

She started to struggle so he set her on her feet. To his astonishment, she quickly regained enough aplomb to straighten her shoulders, face Harlan and declare, "I am totally innocent of any crimes, now or in the past. I don't care what you think you found in that house, I didn't put it there and I have no knowledge of who might have."

Resting a hand lightly on her shoulder, Thad stayed close by and insisted, "It could have been anybody, sheriff. The first prowlers. Whoever ransacked the house later and left the note we gave you. Even one of the people Ben used to work with. A guy named James Reed showed up about a week ago and spent time in the house, too."

"So did you," the sheriff countered.

Thad gaped, speechless. Incensed. Surely Lindy didn't think *he* had had anything to do with all this.

Unfortunately, before she had a chance to speak up to defend him the way he had defended her, Adelaide Crowe stepped in, handcuffed her and hustled her away.

Could Lindy possibly doubt that he had her best interests at heart? No. No way. They might never have discussed personal feelings but she had to know what he thought of her, how he admired her and the amazing job she was doing as a single mother.

Right now, however, Danny was his primary responsibility. He had to explain what was going on and see to it that the child still felt safe, even without Lindy. After that, they'd supervise while a crew from Pearson Products and volunteers from church cleaned up the mess on the lawn.

And later? Thad had no idea. He supposed their pastor, Logan Malloy, would know the right people to call for legal or investigative assistance since Logan had once been a private detective himself.

Beyond that, Thad felt about as lost as his unit had been when they were caught in a haboob—a crippling, blinding dust storm that swept across the Sudan and turned day into night in mere minutes.

Only this was no act of nature, he reminded himself. What was happening to Lindy was all manmade.

Thad scanned the yard as he took out his cell to make the necessary calls. First, he'd ask Logan to round up some muscle, then tell Vernon Betts to bring their largest box truck. Between that and the pickups that so many men in Serenity drove on a regular basis, they'd probably be able to secure Lindy's possessions within a couple hours, three at the most.

And then? Then, he'd make one more call to the number on the business card. If, as he suspected, he got the same mechanical connection he'd gotten before, he was going to tell those idiots that they had gone too far.

Nobody was going to get away with framing an innocent woman.

Not while he was around.

Jail wasn't as bad as Lindy had expected it to be. The tiny cells were clean and except for her, there were no other female prisoners.

"I'll put you on the far end of the women's section so you'll have some privacy. It's Friday. There are bound to be a few drunks picked up tonight and I don't want them to bug you."

"In a dry county?" Lindy asked, surprised when Adelaide laughed aloud.

"Lady, this is the wettest dry county I've ever seen. As long as our citizens can make a run to the Missouri border and bring back booze, we may as well sell the stuff here and keep them off the roads. Not that I approve of drinking, mind you. My daddy was way too fond of John Barleycorn for his own good."

"I didn't hide those drugs in my house," Lindy insisted. "You know that, don't you?"

"Gotta do what the sheriff says." Her expression softened. "Off the record, I figure you were framed. So does your boyfriend."

"I don't have…"

The laugh was louder this time and the deputy's dark eyes sparkled. "Suit yourself. I'll tell you one thing. If I had a man who looked at me the way that Pearson guy looks at you, I'd marry him in a heartbeat. And he's not only handsome, he's nice. Mercy me." She fanned herself with one hand. "Just watchin' him with you was enough to make me blush."

"He didn't…? I didn't…? I mean, when I fainted, we didn't do anything wrong, did we?"

"Not in my book. I thought old Harlan was gonna spit when Thad scooped you up and wouldn't hand you over 'til you came to, though. That is one great guy."

"Yes. He is."

"So, what are you going to do about it?"

Lindy made a face as she focused on the bars separating her from the deputy. "Nothing. I seem to be a little hampered at the moment."

"I meant later."

"Do you really think I'll be released? I know there are times when innocent people spend years in prison before they're finally cleared. Some never are." She blinked back tears of frustration, hoping the other woman didn't think she was trying to elicit sympathy.

Adelaide leaned closer and cupped a hand around her mouth to speak privately. "Just between you and me, we all think those drugs were planted. If we hadn't been called to be there when your stuff was carted out, nobody would have even noticed. Or, the movers would have just helped themselves. Nope. That all came together too perfectly to have been accidental. Somebody set you up."

"Then why am I under arrest?"

"For your safety, among other things. Harlan wants to test the packaging for fingerprints, first, and try to figure out who handled it. Drugs also have chemical clues that can point to their origin or manufacturer. The stuff at your house was high-dollar designer, meaning we have an even better chance of eventually tracing it."

Smiling, the deputy started away. "Try to rest. Lights out is in ten minutes. Your...friend has your little boy so you don't have to worry about him, either."

Lindy nodded, glad to be left alone before the tears started to trickle down her cheeks. She swiped them away, disgusted that her emotions were so close to the surface.

She knew she should be thanking God that Thad had stepped in and taken Danny rather than have him put into foster care or protective custody the way he had been after Ben had beaten him and sent him to the hospital.

Plopping down on the edge of the narrow bed in her cell, Lindy sniffled and closed her eyes, reliving another near disaster—the kidnapping—that had almost cost Danny's life. And her own.

While Danny was recuperating from his father's physical abuse and finding solace in the hospital, cohorts of Ben's had kidnapped them both, as well as Samantha, a nurse who was also Danny's CASA worker. Those horrible men had held them hostage until they were finally rescued amid a hail of gunfire.

At that time, she and Danny had been told they were bait intended to draw Ben out of hiding and make him deliver his ill-gotten gains.

The ploy with them as bait had worked. But when the police had arrived and the shooting had started, Ben had given his life to save their child.

Lindy gasped. She did recall something! The

details were hazy but it seemed to her that those kidnappers had also mentioned something about hidden bank accounts. Could all this be part of the same crime, the same quest? Was she imagining things because she was overwrought or had she blanked that detail out of her mind due to the trauma of seeing her husband die?

Either was possible. The question was whether or not to tell Harlan. Or Thad. Or even James Reed.

In fact, the real dilemma was whether it was safe to trust *anyone*.

TWELVE

During the nearly four hours it took the volunteer crew to haul Lindy's possessions to the Pearson warehouse, Thad had managed to reach an attorney who promised to request bail for her ASAP.

Their pastor had also agreed to contact a few of his old cronies in law enforcement and see what he could find out from them, although he hadn't sounded very hopeful.

Beyond that, Thad was stymied. And angry. And frustrated. And a whole lot more, if he were honest with himself.

How had this situation gotten so out of hand? Was it his fault? He didn't see how it could be, although the tendency to blame himself was hard to set aside.

That same kind of reaction had occurred when he had failed his unit in combat, he realized with a start. As long as he had given his all, had employed every method he knew, there was no way he was actually at fault.

So who was? he asked himself. It was irrational to blame God for the malevolence of humans, yet many did. Perhaps he had even been one of them, at least for a while.

And now? Now, he had concluded that there were factions operating in the world who answered to a different authority, to evil powers that were responsible for a lot of the chaos across the globe. That concept was biblical, no matter what name or names a person attached to the vicious forces.

Thad huffed. "If I get any more metaphysical I'm going to scare myself."

He was a man of action. His first duty was to care for Danny as he had promised, which was one reason why he had allowed the boy to gather up some of his favorite toys and bring them along.

He had also stopped by Hickory Station and bought a simple supper on one of their back-and-forth trips from Pilot Hill Drive to the warehouse.

Danny had acted confused. "What about my mama? Can't she have some, too?"

"Don't worry. The sheriff will feed her. You just concentrate on picking what you'd like and I'll go grab us some milk."

"Soda!" Danny was adamant. "We don't drink milk with pizza."

Thad seriously doubted that a mother who didn't even permit ice cream for dessert would allow soda pop with a meal but he wasn't about to argue.

One sugary drink wouldn't do any lasting harm and he sure didn't want a whimpering kid on his hands. He figured he'd been fortunate to keep the boy calm when he'd seen his mother leaving in the sheriff's car. Since Danny hadn't pitched a fit, then or later, they were probably going to be all right. At least for the present.

The child had stuffed himself, then fallen asleep on the seat of the truck after he'd gotten bored playing video games on his little laptop computer.

When the work of securing Lindy's belongings was completed, Thad reached for Logan's hand to shake it. "Thanks for all the help, Pastor." He waved to others as they started to depart in separate vehicles and called, "Thanks, everybody."

"Our pleasure," Brother Logan replied. "I just wish we were pitching in for a happier reason. Are you sure Danny's going to be okay with you?"

"Positive. His mother wants to keep him out of the legal system again if at all possible."

"There are some wonderful foster parents, you know."

Thad nodded soberly. "I know. I'm just trying to honor Lindy's wishes. Since the gossip mill is so strong in this town, I'm afraid it's just a matter of time until somebody gets in touch with me about relinquishing custody."

"I'll see what I can do to influence the authorities in your favor if it becomes necessary." The pastor clapped Thad on the shoulder. "You are doing okay these days, aren't you?"

"Yes. I've only had one nightmare in the past couple months. That's a big improvement."

"Good. We've been praying for you."

"Thanks."

Realizing how weary he was, Thad heaved a sigh. "Danny's conked out over there in my truck. Do you mind sticking around to watch him while I go lock up? I'll only be a minute."

"No problem. Go. I'll wait right here."

Darkness had already filled the surrounding forest. A halo of artificial light arced over the rear of the metal-clad warehouse and reflected off the windshield of Thad's pickup and the pastor's nearby van.

Thad pulled the chain that lowered the heavy overhead doors. The sound of the links clanking against the mechanism disturbed the otherwise peaceful night.

An owl hooted in the distance.

Coyotes sang a reply.

Securing the chain Thad hurried to the get-in walk door. It swung wide on squeaky hinges. Coyotes yipped again as if answering a summons.

"What can I tell Danny when he wakes up and asks about his mother again?" Thad murmured glancing Heavenward and speaking directly to the Lord. "How am I going to make him understand?"

The short hairs at the nape of his neck suddenly prickled in warning. Everything around him had grown quiet. Too quiet.

He paused to listen, to assess his surroundings more carefully. Knowing that Logan Malloy was also present should have given him peace, only it didn't.

Tensing to battle an unseen enemy, Thad realized there was no sign of the clergyman near the truck. That was more than odd. It was creepy, especially since all the nighttime denizens of the woods had ceased their song at once. It was as if the entire forest was holding its collective breath.

"Brother Logan?" Thad called.

"Over here."

Instead of being close to the truck where Danny dozed, the voice sounded as if it had come from somewhere near the edge of the clearing. Had Danny jumped out of the truck, forcing Logan to run after him?

Thad grabbed the handle on the driver's side and eased open the truck door to check on the boy, relieved to see that he was sound asleep. So, if Logan wasn't chasing Danny, what was he doing?

The pastor jogged back into the circle of light to rejoin Thad. "Did you see him, too?"

"See who?"

"At least one man, on foot, hanging around in the shadows out there. I didn't follow him into the woods because I couldn't be sure he was alone and I needed to stay where I could still watch the boy for you."

"Thanks. Could you tell anything about the guy?"

"Not much. He moved fast, like a young man but that's about all."

"Okay. I'm going to take Danny to my place and keep him safe. You'll see what you can find out for us about the old Southerland case? The sheriff wasn't very helpful."

"He may not know a lot more than he told you," Logan explained. "If federal agencies are involved the chances of their sharing data with local authorities are slim to none. And it's even worse if you're a private detective like I used to be. Unless they need your help, they aren't going to reveal a thing."

Thad nodded. "Speaking of the feds, remember that unlisted number I was given? Do you still have it?"

The slim, dark-haired man patted his jacket pocket. "Right here."

"Good. Just tell your friends to do the best they can identifying that and let me know, will you?"

"Sure. But you should know that considering the opportunities recent technologies provide for avoiding normal channels, that line could connect anywhere. All they'd have to do is run it through a high-powered, sophisticated computer system and it would be virtually untraceable."

"I know. I'm pretty sure it'll turn out to be based in this area, though," Thad said. "Those spooks will want to stick close to Lindy if they really believe she's hiding something."

"You don't think she is, do you?"

"Not for a second. She's a victim of some diabolical scheme and whoever is behind it has the crazy idea she knows where her husband hid a bunch of secret accounts."

"Have you and she brainstormed about it? That might help."

"I'll suggest that. Once we get her out of jail." He raked his fingers through his short hair, showing his frustration. "I can't believe anybody would buy the idea that Lindy Southerland is using or dealing drugs. I have never met a sweeter, more honest person in my entire life."

Logan began to smile. "You don't say."

"Yes, I do say. And don't look at me like that. I'm just helping out a victim who happened to cross my path, that's all."

"Okay, if you insist." He gestured to the truck where the child still napped. "I'll keep you and Lindy and Danny in my prayers. Good night."

"Good night. Thanks again."

Climbing behind the wheel and shutting the door as quietly as possible, Thad turned the key.

The sputtering engine noise was finally enough to awaken the seven-year-old. He sat up and rubbed his eyes. "Where are we?"

"Just leaving the factory. Go back to sleep."

"Where's…?"

Thad could tell the child was pausing to remember the details of their situation.

"I want my mama."

"Maybe tomorrow," Thad said, silently vowing to do something, anything, to get Lindy out of custody.

Danny began to sniffle noisily. "She needs to kiss me good-night and tuck me in."

It occurred to Thad to offer to stand in for Danny's mother. He dismissed the notion out of hand. He wasn't the affectionate type. It just wasn't his nature to be nurturing, which was one more good reason why he'd let others adopt his brother's kids without putting up a legal fight.

Instead, he reached over and gave the boy a manly pat on the knee. "Hang in there kid. You'll be okay. Nobody ever tucked me in and I'm just fine."

The child scooted as close to Thad as his safety belt would allow, reached out and gently touched his arm as he said, "That's sad."

If there had been a chance of speaking without a hitch in his voice Thad might have argued.

However, he knew better than to try. The boy's simple show of affection and empathy had touched him too deeply.

Night in Serenity was just as the town's name promised—serene. Lindy wouldn't have minded the peace and quiet if it had not given her far too much opportunity to think.

"Okay, to *fret,*" she grumbled in disgust. What she was doing was far more than mere thinking. It was worrying to the nth degree. She knew better. She should be giving thanks that Thad was looking after Danny and that he had arranged to safeguard her possessions, too, but it wasn't easy to focus on the positive when so many negative aspects kept occurring to her.

She heaved a sigh. "Well, you really did it this time, didn't you, Ben," she whispered, speaking to the dimness of the empty cell while envisioning the man to whom she had once pledged her life. This whole mess led straight back to him. It had to.

Between the quest for Ben's so-called stash and the presence of drugs in her home, there was little doubt her late husband had set this disaster in motion. He might be long gone but she was apparently still paying for his folly.

Pacing seemed to help calm her so Lindy circled the small cell repeatedly. She was going around and around all right. Had been since that day when those men had broken into her house and messed with her credit cards.

Although the house might be her greatest financial concern it was still just a building. The important thing, the only thing that truly mattered, was her little boy. As long as Danny was kept safe and sound, she could face any kind of future.

Even one in prison? she asked herself. That concept gave her the shivers and made her stomach lurch. She didn't even want to think of such an unfair fate, yet she supposed it was possible that whoever had framed her would keep up the attacks indefinitely.

Which meant that Danny was in as much jeopardy as she was, she reasoned, tasting bile in the back of her throat and wondering if she was going to be literally ill. Adelaide had intimated that locking her up was for her own good. If that was the case, then shouldn't her little boy be in there with her, at least for the night?

"No. Of course not," she answered cynically. "But it sure would be nice to talk to him, to tell him I'm all right and assure him it's safe to stay with Thad."

Yearning for her son overcame Lindy and nearly made her weep. *Poor Danny. First he loses his father and now me.*

No matter how illogical that conclusion was or how much being removed from Ben's negative influence had benefited the child, she knew Danny missed his daddy. Danny was closer to her than he'd ever been to Ben—he must be missing her, too. And as the only surviving parent, she believed it was her job to prepare her son to face adult life. How could she do that if they were kept apart, maybe for years?

Lindy stopped pacing and grabbed the cell bars. No one had offered to let her use the phone. Wasn't that her right? Movies about police procedures portrayed it that way. It certainly wouldn't hurt to ask.

She tried a simple "Hello?"

The hallway remained deserted, darkened except for the glow from a small exit sign. Below that, the door leading to the main office was shut.

"Adelaide? Deputy Crowe? Are you out there?" Lindy paused and listened. There was no reply.

The next breath was deeper and the shout a little shaky. "Hello? Can anybody hear me?"

A distant male voice hooted. "I hear ya, darlin'. You come to spring me? Huh?"

Well, the male side of the jail seemed to be occupied, as predicted. So if other prisoners could hear her, why didn't a deputy answer?

"Sheriff?"

Lindy realized she was starting to sound panicky. That wasn't good. If there was something wrong out there, the last thing she wanted to do was play the part of a victim.

The door at the end of the hall creaked open enough to permit a narrow shaft of brighter light from the office.

Lindy held her breath. No one spoke. No one entered. The door didn't move any farther.

Finally, unable to contain her anxiety, Lindy shouted at the top of her lungs, "Hey! I want my phone call."

A shadow broke the beam of bright light for a second.

Struggling to see better, Lindy pressed her right cheek against the bars and peered down the narrow hallway.

The silhouette shifted. There was a metallic sound as an object hit the floor then started to roll across the bare concrete.

Visions of an attack filled Lindy's mind.

Moments before the door slammed and shut out the brightness, she thought she had glimpsed a dull-looking canister on the floor.

By the time her eyes adjusted to the change in the light level, she was positive she could smell smoke.

A hissing sound resonated. Whitish clouds billowed toward her cell, blotting out the glow from the exit sign.

Lindy screamed. Coughed. Began to wheeze.

Trapped!

There was no escape. No way to keep from breathing the noxious fumes.

All Lindy could think to do was bury her face in her pillow and pray that the gas was not lethal.

She envisioned her only child. Holding Danny's hand was a tall, strong man. The kind of man her son should have had for a father. Thad Pearson.

The images of man and boy looked at her.

Together, they smiled.

The pure sweetness of that make-believe scene caused a flood of tears.

And that moisture on the pillowcase made it a tiny bit easier to draw a shallow, filtered breath.

THIRTEEN

The sounds of sirens in the distance alerted Thad that something was amiss.

Slowing the truck's speed, he checked his mirrors. Fire engines were fast approaching from the rear, their red-and-white lights flashing and horns honking.

He pulled to the curb near the courthouse to let them pass, then started to drive away as soon as the road was clear.

"I wanna watch the fire trucks!" Danny exclaimed. "Please, can we? Please?"

"Sorry, no. We're not supposed to get in the firemen's way," Thad replied.

"But they're right over there. See?" He unclasped his seat belt and got onto his knees. "Please, please, please? I wanna watch Timmy and Paul's new daddy shooting water."

That mention of his orphaned nephews made Thad's gut clench. Paying closer attention to the place where the firefighters were rapidly deploying tied his insides in a knot the size of a basketball. Thad parked his truck on the shoulder and turned off the engine.

Smoke was rolling out of the small sheriff's office.

The jail was in that building.

Lindy was in that building! Grabbing his keys and quickly jumping out, he hollered, "Come on."

Danny was already scooting toward him across the seat. As Thad reached for him, he launched his small self into the man's arms and held onto his neck.

"Good boy," Thad told him, trying to sound calm when he wanted to shout and break into a run. "As soon as I find somebody we know to look after you, I'll go see if I can help."

"I thought you said we were supposed to stay away."

"This is different." His voice grew stern, commanding. "Just do as I say. Understand?"

Danny's reply of okay was more of a whimper than a word.

"Hey, sorry I sounded grumpy. I'm not mad at you, all right?"

The child nodded. "Where are we going?"

"Right over here with these other people," Thad explained, frantically scanning the gathering, milling crowd on the courthouse lawn. If he couldn't find someone he knew and trusted to watch

Danny, he was going to have to take his own advice and let the firefighters handle the emergency.

"Which one is Tim and Paul's daddy?" the boy asked.

Thad barely heard the query. All his concentration was focused on finding a trustworthy man or woman to look after the little boy in his arms. Lindy trusted him to safeguard her son and he intended to do so. The problem was, he couldn't rescue the mother and keep her child out of danger at the same time.

"Please, God, please," Thad murmured. "Send me somebody. Anybody."

Danny let go with one hand and began to wave happily. Following the child's line of sight, Thad spotted Louise Williams, one of his employees. *Perfect.*

He wove his way through the throng and greeted the wiry, middle-age woman. "Louise. Glad you're here. Can you mind Danny for me for a few minutes?"

"Sure." She pulled her sweater closer and shivered. "Where's his jacket?"

"I don't know." Thad was already setting the boy on his feet next to her. "Just watch him, okay?"

"Sure, but, where are you…"

Her voice faded as mayhem reigned. Firefighters were shouting into their handheld radios or calling to each other in person. Pumps were starting to rumble as they cranked them up to higher pressure to supply the hoses. The hum of the gathered casual observers was punctuated with overly excited bursts of exclamations.

Thad pushed his way to the front of the crowd and grabbed the arm of the first uniformed man he saw. It was Levi Kelso, the police chief.

"What's going on?" Thad demanded.

"Don't know yet." He regarded Thad the way a person might look at a pestering gnat. "Get back and let the pros handle this."

"Did you get the prisoners out?"

"Yes. Of course." He frowned. "Why?"

"Because I don't see Lindy."

"Who?"

Thad was so frantic he almost yelled. "Lindy Southerland. Harlan arrested her this evening."

Turning away, the chief spoke into his radio, then frowned. Thad heard him say, "All right. As soon as you can," before looking up.

"My men didn't know we had a female prisoner," Levi explained, "and the dispatcher was only half conscious when we carried her outside. So she was in no condition to mention it, either. We evacuated the male side of the jail right away, but…"

Thad grabbed the man's arm. "Lindy's still in there?"

"Don't worry. We'll have her out in a few minutes. Some joker apparently made a false accident report to lure everybody away and empty the station, then set off a smoke bomb inside. We don't think there's a real fire."

Unconvinced, Thad burst through the line and followed the fire hoses through the main door and into the shared offices of police and sheriff. All the nearby interior doors stood open and a firemen wearing full breathing apparatus's were setting up a large fan near the front.

Thad immediately began to struggle for air. His throat burned. The deep, racking cough that followed was so strong it made his sides ache.

He peered through the smoky atmosphere, hoping to see one of the deputies he knew. Apparently, everyone had evacuated. So how was he going to locate Lindy?

As soon as he'd seen the smoke, he'd suspected that this might be another attack on her. If he went with that gut feeling, the smoke should be thickest wherever she was being housed. It was an idea worth pursuing.

Eyes tearing, lungs screaming for cleaner air, Thad pivoted in the smoky office. Most of the problem seemed to be centered to the right, down a corridor he could barely see. That was where he'd go. That was where he'd find her. He knew it.

He rammed a hip into the edge of a desk and nearly tripped over a loop of heavy canvas fire hose before he reached that doorway. Another man or woman in full firefighting gear had picked up a smoking canister about the size of one of the Pearson rolling pins and was carrying it out in a gloved hand.

"Out of the way." The man's voice sounded muffled behind the protective mask. "You shouldn't be in here."

Thad took a deeper breath to answer and was overcome with coughing once again. By the time he was able to speak, the firefighter had passed him and was carrying the canister out into the street.

"Lindy!" Thad managed to choke out. "Where are you?"

No one answered.

Groping along the wall he felt for bars. There. He reached forward. And again.

"Lindy!"

Feet sliding sideways, his hands moving from bar to bar along the grates, he kept going. Now that the source of the smoke had been removed and the fan was blowing, the air was beginning to clear a little.

The whirling lights of the engines outside were throwing intermittent flashes through a small, high window at the end of the cellblock. That was all the light Thad had. It was enough.

He found her in the last cell. She was on her

knees beside her bunk with her face pressed into her bed pillow.

"Lindy!" he shouted, hearing the pathos in his voice as he wondered if she was still breathing.

She didn't move.

Thad heard footsteps behind him.

"Over here," he yelled. "Bring a key!"

The shoulder that pushed him out of the way was clad in a police uniform but also wearing one of the fire department's regulation air-packs units. Thad thought it might be John Waltham but he wasn't sure.

The lock clicked. Before the door was fully open, Thad sidled through.

Fell to his knees beside Lindy. Touched her shoulder. Called her name. She didn't react.

Not waiting for help, he scooped her up and turned to leave.

Officer Waltham took off his mask and placed it over her face, staying close so he and Thad could move as one and give Lindy the full advantage of the purer air.

They were outside in mere seconds.

An ambulance was waiting.

Thad went directly to the paramedics and handed her over, then bent double to continue coughing.

"We'd better take you in, too," one of the medics said.

"Just take care of her," Thad managed to say between bouts of wheezing and hacking. "Is she breathing?"

"Yeah. She's already coming around. Looks like she'll be fine. We need to take her to the E.R. to be sure but I wouldn't worry."

Gasping and red-eyed from the smoke, Thad swiped at the moisture on his cheeks, hoping everyone would assume it was caused by irritation.

All he knew for sure was that his relief at hearing that Lindy was conscious was so great it was almost overwhelming.

One of the paramedics tried to guide him to the ambulance.

He resisted. "No. I can't leave. I have to get Danny."

"Whoever he is, I'm sure he'll be fine while you get some oxygen. Just sit with us for a bit and let us help you."

"No."

Thad jerked his arm free and stepped away from the ambulance. His vision was blurry, his eyes burning from the acrid smoke.

He pivoted, trying to search the crowd. Where had Louise been when he'd last seen her? There? Maybe more over that way?

At a loss, he turned back to the medics. "Can you wash my eyes out? I can't see."

"Sure. Over here. I'll need you to sign a release if you refuse further treatment, anyway."

Bending at the waist, Thad turned his head to the right and let cool water bathe his burning eyes as the medic slowly poured it. Then, they did the same for the other side and handed him a towel.

"That's better. Thanks."

Again, he studied the spectators. Considering how attached Danny was to his mother, and to him, he expected to see the boy pulling Louise's arm and leading her closer.

He didn't see the older woman or the child at first. Then, he saw Louise weaving through the crowd.

An officer stopped her from coming closer.

Thad could see her waving her hands and speaking but he couldn't make out what she was saying.

Apparently satisfied that she should be let through the barricades, the deputy stepped aside and pointed toward the ambulance.

Blotting his still stinging eyes, Thad wiped his face with the towel. When he lowered it Louise was standing in front of him. Danny wasn't with her.

"Where *is* he?" Thad demanded.

She was wringing her hands. "I don't know. He said he was cold so I let him go back to your truck for his jacket. He promised he'd come right back but he never did."

"How long ago was that?"

"Just a few minutes. I told Harlan and Adelaide and they've already started a search."

Thad was beside himself. He'd thought it was safe to leave the boy with another responsible adult. The choice had been his. He'd desperately wanted to rescue Lindy, and he had, but if that decision had cost her her son, she'd never forgive him.

Gritting his teeth and trying to suppress another coughing fit, Thad realized that he would never forgive himself, either.

That little boy meant more to him than life itself.

Danny saw the menacing-looking men standing next to Thad's truck. Two of them. And they seemed familiar. Where had he seen them before? *In the house. That night when Mama and I hid behind the couch.* He'd never forget those mean faces or the way they had yelled at him and his mother. It was *so* scary.

One of the men, the taller one, turned his head in Danny's direction.

The boy felt as if his sneakers were nailed to the courthouse lawn. He wanted to yell. To run. To hide. But his body refused to move.

The tall man pointed. "There he is."

Danny wished he could melt into the ground

and disappear. His mouth felt dry. He knew he was trembling.

A heavier, meaner-looking guy was circling the truck and both of the men were starting to come his way.

Run! Run! Now! his instincts screamed.

He tried to lift one foot. Nothing happened. The men seemed to be moving in slow motion, edging closer and closer.

Try harder, something inside him insisted. *Go find Thad.*

Thoughts of seeking sanctuary with the ex-marine were strong enough to enable Danny to break free.

He whirled. Started to run.

Behind him, someone yelled, "Get him!"

That only spurred more speed. More agility.

Ducking and weaving between spectators who had gathered in response to the sirens, Danny felt as if his feet were flying, barely touching the ground.

He knew he didn't dare stop. But where was Thad? Was he still helping the firemen?

Danny bobbed. He cut right, then left, then right again, never daring to slow down enough to look back. Nobody had to tell him the men were still chasing him. He could feel them back there even if he couldn't hear them anymore.

A bright spotlight suddenly blinded him. Someone called his name.

Danny kept running.

Running for his life.

Looking for the one man he knew he could trust.

His eyes widened. There! Was that Thad? It had
to be.

Gasping and nearly spent, the child altered his
forward course just enough to bring him into line
with his goal. He didn't slow until he'd rammed
into Thad. Grabbing him around the knees, Danny
began to sob.

"Easy, son, easy," the man soothed. "I've got
you. You're safe."

He let himself be pried loose and lifted into his
rescuer's arms.

He had never been more terrified in his whole
life.

And he had never felt safer than he did right
now.

Lindy was resting in the ambulance with a small
oxygen mask over her nose and mouth when she
saw Thad approach carrying her son.

They both seemed to be the worse for wear yet
had never looked more dear.

She lifted the clear plastic mask and smiled.
"Hi, fellas. Nice night for a little excitement, don't
you think?"

Noting that Thad was wheezing and Danny was taking shuddering breaths as if he had been crying, she scowled. "What's up? I know where *I've* been. Where have you two been?"

"I carried you out of the jail," Thad explained. "You were unconscious when I found you but the medics said you'll be fine."

Lindy tried to suppress a cough and failed. "Then I owe you my thanks. Again." Her reddened eyes widened. "Wait a minute. Where was Danny while you were rescuing me?"

"I left him with Louise Williams, from work."

Lindy could tell there was more to it than he was admitting but she was too weary to insist on an immediate explanation. "Good. I'd like you to continue to look after him for me. Please? They tell me I'm going to be sent to the hospital. If Samantha's on duty tonight and I see her there, I want to be able to tell her she doesn't need to notify Family Services."

"No problem. Danny and I will follow in a little while and see if they'll let us visit you. In the meantime, I intend to find out just what happened here."

"I think I saw something like a smoke bomb or maybe tear gas. It was tossed through the door from the main office and there was no way I could keep from breathing the fumes."

"We know. The fire department has the device."

Lindy watched her self-appointed guardian draw a shaky breath, then force a smile. She knew he was thinking the same thing she was—that this had been another attack specifically aimed at her. The question was *why?*

Pausing to take another deep breath from her mask she finally said, "This doesn't fit with the other things that have happened to me. I mean, why gas me? They'd already succeeded in framing me for drugs, emptying my bank account, ruining my credit and evicting me from my house. What else could they hope to accomplish?"

Seeing the way Thad's arms tightened around her son, she was suddenly aware that the child was acting strangely. He wasn't merely upset. He was behaving as if he was scared to death.

"Mama's going to be okay, honey. Don't worry," Lindy said to reassure him.

When the boy remained mute and buried his face against Thad's shoulder, she grew more suspicious that something else was wrong.

As her gaze met Thad's and held it, she was positive.

He cleared his throat, turned aside to cough, then faced her again. She could tell from his expression that he was about to reveal a secret. She just hoped she was up to hearing whatever he had to say.

"I think they were either after you or Danny, or

maybe both," he said quietly. "He told me he spotted the guys who broke into your house and swore they were chasing him. I didn't see anybody but it's possible he's right just the same."

Before she could fully accept Thad's statement, he added something even more ominous.

"I've told the sheriff what I think and he's agreed to let you stay in the hospital overnight. You'll have a guard posted at your door. That's more to keep somebody else out than it is to keep you in. Harlan doesn't really believe you were selling or using drugs. He just has to follow the letter of the law."

"So I'll be lying there, totally exposed to danger, while the police pretend to be watching me?"

"I wouldn't put it quite that way," Thad replied. "I'm sure they'll do their jobs."

Lindy couldn't help sounding a little bitter when she said, "You mean like they did their jobs when Ben was shot?" She gave a harsh-sounding chuckle that ended in another coughing fit.

"Would you like me to stay at the hospital, too?" Thad asked.

She wanted to tell him *yes,* but doing so would mean that her innocent child would also be exposed to possible danger. Therefore, she did what any good mother would have done. She said no with as much conviction as she could muster.

The way Lindy saw it, the only way things could

get worse for her at this point was if something bad happened to her only child.

Keeping Danny safe and sound had always been her job. She wasn't going to change her mind about that now, no matter what happened to her.

FOURTEEN

It was hard for Thad to entrust Lindy to the care of a sheriff's deputy but the fact that it was Adelaide Crowe who had been assigned the duty helped him accept it. That young officer was not only sharp-witted, she was savvy. Nobody with ulterior motives was going to get past her.

After assuring Lindy that his breathing was okay, he had taken Danny home with him and managed to talk the boy into going to sleep by agreeing to "camp" in the living room in sleeping bags. There was enough adventure and fun involved in doing that to placate the child and still allow Thad to get some needed shut-eye.

By morning he felt rested, although his nerves were still on edge. A quick phone call to Lindy's room would let him know she was all right and hopefully help untie some of the knots in his neck and shoulders.

"Morning," he said as soon as she answered the bedside phone. "How are you?"

"Better, thanks." Her voice sounded muted and he suspected she was cupping a hand around the receiver. "I still have my babysitter at the door, though."

"Adelaide?"

"For another hour or so. Then she goes off duty and they'll give me someone else, I guess."

"We'll be by to visit before that." He felt a tug on his sleeve. "Here. Somebody else wants to talk to you."

Listening to the boy's side of the conversation, Thad could tell that Lindy was cautioning him to be good because he kept nodding his tousled head and murmuring, "Uh-huh. Uh-huh, I will." Finally, he handed the phone back.

"We're going to go out for breakfast," Thad said. "Is there anything we can bring you or are you loving the hospital food?"

"A sweet roll and coffee would be wonderful. And make sure Danny wears his jacket. It's cold outside."

"Okay. Look for us in about half an hour or forty-five minutes. I thought I'd take my little buddy to Hickory Station where we first met."

"Fine." Her voice gentled. "And, thank you, Thad."

"My pleasure. He's a great kid."

Bidding Lindy goodbye, he realized how much he'd meant what he'd said about Danny. They were getting along very well, in spite of the scary episode the night before, and thankfully he hadn't had any combat dreams while the boy had been in his care.

"I wanna go see my mama," Danny piped up.

"We will. First we'll go get breakfast, like I told her, and then you can take her some goodies from the restaurant."

"Yeah! I love doughnuts!"

"You can eat some this one time. It might be best if that was our little secret, though. I don't think your mother approves of too many sweets."

It made Thad smile to recall that Lindy had asked him to bring her a sweet roll. She might have rules for Danny's healthful diet but there were clearly times when those rules were broken on her own behalf, particularly when she was facing a tray of bland hospital food.

He'd have to pick up an extra treat or two for Adelaide or whoever took over for her, too. There were plenty of stale jokes about cops loving doughnuts but that didn't mean it wasn't true.

Grinning, he locked up his apartment, ushered the child to the truck and made sure he was safely belted in.

Clearly, Danny was excited about the prospect of seeing his mother again, although that didn't mean he hadn't also brought along an armload of the toys he'd salvaged from his room at home.

Thad's smile broadened even more and he felt his cheeks warming as he slid behind the wheel and fired up the truck. Danny wasn't the only one who could hardly wait to visit Lindy.

A certain ex-marine was pretty eager to do so, too.

The morning was creeping by. Lindy glanced at the clock on the wall at the foot of her bed. What was keeping her two guys?

She huffed in self-deprecation. *Two?* Last time she'd looked, there was only one who belonged to her. Danny. The grown man was another story, one she felt was still being written.

Thad might keep insisting he wouldn't make a good father but that didn't make it so. She knew better. She had seen him with Danny. Had repeatedly watched their interaction with a lump in her throat. They were so well suited to each other it was amazing.

Did that mean that *she* was the real problem? Maybe. Or perhaps Thad just didn't want to commit to anyone. She certainly wouldn't blame him if he avoided getting tangled up in her confusing life more than he already was. Any man who considered marrying her had to be more than brave. He had to be a little foolhardy.

The door to her room swung open.

Lindy beamed, assuming she knew who was

entering bearing the enormous bouquet of flowers that hid his face.

How sweet.

She leaned to look on either side of her visitor. Where was her son?

About to ask, she sat up straighter, got a glimpse of the bearer of the flowers and almost gasped.

"Good morning, Lindy," James Reed said smoothly. He put the vase on a side table and stepped back, smiling. "I was sorry to hear you'd had an accident."

Speechless, she frowned and stared. How did Reed know about her being in the hospital? Who had told him? And why would he care enough to drive all the way to Serenity to visit her? They had no real connection anymore, not after Ben's sick leave payments had ended and she had rejected Reed's theory that they might share a reward for finding hidden bank accounts.

"I can see you're surprised to see me," the suave businessman said. "Let me explain."

Stepping back from the array of blossoms, she saw that he was holding something. Something dark and fairly small with sharp angles and a hand grip.

He swiveled and pointed the barrel of the gun at her while laying the index finger of his other hand across his lips. "Shh. You don't want to be responsible for getting that pretty cop I saw out in the hallway hurt, now do you?"

Lindy shook her head. Her hands drew folds of the bedcovers into her fists and twisted them.

That was her only tangible hold on reality, on her turbulent emotions. If she called out or screamed in terror, Adelaide would come bursting through the door to be greeted by a bullet from Reed's gun. Lindy had seen that kind of failed rescue attempt before when Ben had tried to save her and Danny. She was not going to contribute to anyone else's death. Not knowingly.

"I'm glad to see we understand each other," Reed said, pocketing the firearm. He approached and perched a hip on the edge of her bed, just out of reach. "Now, you and I are going to have a little chat, Mrs. Southerland. If you tell me what I want to know, I'll disappear and you'll never see me again. I hear the Caymans are lovely this time of year."

Lindy bit her lip to help control herself. All she wanted to do was get rid of him, one way or another. "How, how can I help you when Ben didn't tell me a thing?"

"I'm sure you'll think of a way." He gave her a snide smile that didn't reach his eyes.

The menace in his expression was as frightening as the gun had been—maybe more so.

Racking her brain for something—anything—

that would send him on a wild-goose chase and get him out of the hospital, Lindy was praying silently when she saw the door start to move again.

It swung open.

Reed stood and backed off.

Danny burst in, raced across the room and scrambled onto her bed with a joyous, "Mama!"

Lindy took him in her arms and pulled him close. Held tight. Kept praying wordlessly.

Her gaze met Thad's and locked. She desperately wanted him to take Danny and go away. If she revealed that she was in danger, she knew he'd try to rescue her. And then what would happen to her little boy?

Hide your feelings, her instinct insisted. *Don't let him see how scared you are.*

When Lindy tried to smile, she could tell it was too late. Thad's expression was already wary and growing more guarded by the second. His attention was so focused on her, she wondered if he'd even noticed that James Reed was also in the room.

"Thad and me, we brought doughnuts, Mama," Danny said happily.

She eyed the paper sack and take-out coffee container in the man's hand. "I can see that. Thank you. Now get going or you'll be late for school."

"There's no school on Saturday," the child told her. "Silly you."

"You should still be going," Lindy insisted.

Her eyes were drawn back to Thad's face. In his expression she read a multitude of emotions including concern. As the seconds ticked by, however, that concern was rapidly being replaced by determination and what she could only assume was the readiness to fight even though he had not even acknowledged that Reed was present.

"Tell you what," Thad said calmly as he placed the coffee and the sack on Lindy's bedside tray. "We'll give your mother her sweet roll and then you can take the doughnuts out to the lady police officer like we planned."

Danny slid backward off the bed, feet first. He was beaming as if he'd just been given a wonderful gift. "Okay. The big one's for Mama, right?"

"Right." Thad withdrew the cinnamon roll and placed it on a napkin before closing the sack and handing it to the boy. "Tell Deputy Crowe that these are all for her but it's okay if she wants to share with you."

"Okay."

"And while you're eating, stay in the hallway so you don't get your mother's bed sticky. Understand?"

"Okay." Danny was off at a run.

To Lindy's relief the door swung closed and stayed that way.

"Now," Thad said firmly, "suppose you tell me

what's going on." He gestured toward the man he had thus far ignored. "What's he doing here?"

"I just brought Mrs. Southerland some flowers," Reed said smoothly. "Shouldn't you be going too?"

Lindy's pounding heart felt as if it had lodged in her throat when Thad said, "Not until I find out what's really happening here."

"My business is with Mrs. Southerland, not you."

Thad shook his head and stepped between Lindy and her other visitor. "Wrong," he said with obvious rancor. "Anything you have to say to her you'd better be ready to say to me, too."

"Aah, so that's how it is. I should have guessed a pretty widow with millions in the bank wouldn't be alone for long."

Lindy found her voice. "Will you *stop* it. I do not have money. I can't even bail myself out of the financial mess somebody has forced on me."

"That would be our friends in government," Reed said, almost purring with satisfaction. "I know all about that. They were stupid enough to approach me recently and ask me to stop sending you checks." He smiled snidely. "It was then that I realized just how much I'd overlooked after Ben's death."

"Well, they're wrong," Lindy insisted. "I don't

have a spare dime. Did it occur to any of you that maybe Ben never hid anything?"

"Oh, but he did," Reed insisted. "The feds got as far as learning about his offshore accounts, they just can't access them without the right numbers and passwords. You have those, Lindy, whether you realize it or not."

She was dumbfounded. Could she really have what he wanted and not know it? Was that possible? Her head spun. Was there anything Ben had said in the past that might indicate where the answers lay?

Thad's voice rumbled, drawing her back to the present. "I take it you don't intend to turn those funds over to the feds."

"Smart man." Reed chuckled. "I was hoping there might be a hidden program on Ben's old hard drive but I figure, if the best techs the DEA has can't find it, it's not there. Same goes for the lady's laptop."

"What do you know about my laptop?" Lindy asked.

"I had my men download all your files when they broke into your house. Remember?"

"That was how you got my banking information?"

"Of course. I helped myself to what I needed before I turned an altered copy over to my so-called friends in the government. They were none the wiser."

"You falsified the payment records on my house, too?"

Shaking his head, Reed laughed again. "No. I can't take credit for that. It was the big boys who had you tossed out into the street and framed for drug possession."

"They wouldn't do that," Thad insisted.

Reed's smile remained. "You think not?"

"But, *why?*" Lindy asked. "What can they hope to gain? If they wanted my help, why didn't they just ask for it?"

"Probably because they believe you're guilty, too," Thad told her as he took her hand. "I should have realized that a plan so far-reaching had to have originated with people who have a lot of power and influence."

Lindy looked back and forth between the two men. This entire fiasco was so improbable it was hard to grasp, let alone accept as truth.

One thing and one thing only was certain. Reed had a gun in his pocket and Thad didn't know about it. The best outcome she could hope for at this point was that no one would get killed before everything was settled.

Thad could tell Lindy was afraid, and well she should be, given what they had just learned. Yet her uneasiness seemed to be focused on Reed himself rather than simply on his words.

She kept glancing back and forth with those beautiful green eyes of hers as if she could somehow impart her innermost thoughts. Thad wanted to read her mind, he just didn't know where to begin. If only she would give him a clue.

When she smiled pointedly at him and said, "Well, thanks for coming by," as if she expected him to leave, he was stunned. Surely she didn't think he'd consider abandoning her to the machinations of James Reed? Or did she?

"Take Danny home and don't let him eat too many doughnuts, okay?"

Thad nodded soberly. *Now* she was making sense. Thanks to the stress of the past few minutes, he'd totally forgotten that they had the boy to consider. Of course Lindy wanted Danny away from there, particularly since Reed had just admitted complicity in the plots to ruin her.

Torn, Thad squeezed her hand. "Are you sure that's what you want?"

Since his back was turned to the other man, he used his eyes to signal his deep concern. If Lindy sent him away he'd have to go, at least long enough to see to it that Danny was safe. He wouldn't like it, but he'd heed her wishes.

"Yes. Please?"

The quaver in her voice cut him to the quick.

He knew how scared she was. The question was, could he just walk away?

Suppose he stayed? Thad asked himself. What could Reed do about it? Perhaps that question was worth pursuing before he left the room.

As he studied Lindy's face, he realized that his hesitation was pushing her to the brink of her already tenuous self-control. Why? He was bigger and stronger than the businessman so what was making her think he couldn't simply overpower him and settle things once and for all?

Suddenly realizing what might be frightening her so much, Thad squeezed her hand to draw her attention to it, then formed his into the shape of a pistol and arched his eyebrows for a second as he withdrew.

Eyes widening, she nodded just enough to provide his answer. *Reed was armed.* If there was any kind of altercation in the hospital, many innocent bystanders could be hurt or killed. Lindy was making the courageous choice to clear the room and he could not argue with her logic.

"All right," Thad said, working to keep his voice even in spite of the fact that his heart was about to break. "We'll see you later."

She blinked back tears, almost making him change his mind. He understood her motives. But that didn't mean he had to like what she was doing. If only there was some way to tell what kind of weapon Reed had— and whether he had come to the hospital alone.

There was that possibility to consider, too, Thad reasoned. They already knew that Reed had hired a couple thugs to break into Lindy's house and copy her computer files. What was to say he hadn't brought backup muscle with him this morning? Reed's smug smirk seemed to confirm that.

Pausing to gaze into her lovely face one last time, Thad wished he could bend and kiss her goodbye.

Doing so would be more than foolish, he decided easily. Right now, Reed didn't know how much he and Lindy meant to each other and that was the way it must stay.

Once their foes realized what was in Thad's heart, and hopefully also in Lindy's, they would have another bargaining chip to hold over her head. Knowing that she loved her son with all her heart was bad enough.

Nevertheless, he wanted her to know how he felt. Even if she didn't return his affection he needed her to know.

In the back of his mind was the suspicion that he might lose her forever. He refused to acknowledge those murmurings. Lindy would get out of this. He would get her out of this. Somehow.

But until that happened he had one important

fact to impart. Waiting until he was sure she was paying full attention, he mouthed a silent *I love you*.

Then, he turned and strode out of the room.

FIFTEEN

Lindy could hardly breathe. Hardly function, let alone think clearly. She knew she had done the right thing by sending Thad away. She just felt so alone now. So abandoned. So vulnerable. She couldn't even bring herself to be happy about Thad's last, unspoken words.

Had he really indicated that he loved her? It seemed so. Unless, of course, her imagination was playing tricks on her because that was exactly what she'd wanted him to say.

Reed sidled up to the foot of her bed once again. "Smart lady."

So angry she was speechless, Lindy glared at him.

"All right. This is what's going to happen," he said flatly. "There's going to be a disturbance in another part of the hospital in a few minutes. As soon as your guard is called away to assist her fellow officers, you and I are going to walk out of here."

"I can't just leave like that. I'm under arrest," Lindy countered.

"Yes, you are. And a drug dealer like you would be highly likely to make a break for it the minute she had the chance." He grinned slyly. "That was the plan in the first place."

"*You* put the smoke bomb in the jail?"

"Not personally," he said. "But I did arrange to have it done. I had to get you out of there so you and I could have a private chat."

Lindy's thoughts raced. She knew her chances of survival were minimal once she and Reed were away from the others, yet what else could she do? How could she hope to leave enough clues for anyone—for Thad—to follow her?

"Where are we going to go?" she asked, trying to maintain a modicum of composure.

"I have a plane waiting at the airport."

"What airport? The little runway down by Pearson Products?"

"Yes."

That was a surprise. The Serenity airport was hardly more than a paved strip of asphalt with numbers painted at the ends and a stripe down the center. There was so little air traffic there that she had only noticed one or two small private planes coming and going in all the time she'd worked for Thad.

Reed chuckled. "I can tell you don't believe me.

You'll see for yourself soon enough." Slipping a hand into his jacket pocket, he gestured with the gun through the cloth. "Get dressed. We need to be ready to leave as soon as the ruckus starts."

She gritted her teeth. "I'm not doing anything of the kind in front of you. Turn around."

"Not in a million years, lady. Take your clothes into the bathroom if you're embarrassed. I'll wait here."

As Lindy complied, her mind was racing. There had to be some way to escape. Something she had overlooked that would enable her to flee.

Casting her gaze around the small bathroom while she donned jeans and a sweater beneath her denim jacket, she noted that it didn't even have a window, let alone another normal exit.

There was only one way out.

Right into the arms of James Reed.

While she'd been dressing, Lindy had had little time to leave clues and even fewer ways to do so. If she'd had her purse, she figured she could have written on the bathroom mirror with lipstick. Too bad no one had bothered to bring it to her after her arrest.

The only thing at hand that would leave a mark was the tiny tube of toothpaste she'd been issued as a patient. Squeezing a dab onto her finger she tested it on the mirror. The marks it left weren't bright or easy to read but maybe that was just as well. If her captor glanced into the room he might not see that the smears she was leaving were clues.

Making a *P.P.* for Pearson Products used up so much of the bluish gel she realized she wouldn't have nearly enough to explain what was going on.

The door rattled as if Reed was coming in.

"I'm almost ready. Just give me a couple more seconds."

What else could she write? How could she squeeze out enough more gel to spell "airport"?

She couldn't. The only thing that might help was if she could make a smear that looked like an airplane.

It didn't help that her hand was shaking. The so-called airplane resembled a sideways letter *T* more than it did a plane. Taken aback, she suddenly realized that the object also looked like a cross.

Reminded that she had been so frightened she had failed to pray the way she should have, Lindy closed her eyes, took a deep, settling breath and began to turn her life, her future, her loved ones, over to the Lord.

Thad hadn't wasted time chatting with Adelaide other than to ask when she was expecting to be relieved of duty. He did want to warn her but he was afraid doing so would trigger an all-out assault on Lindy's hospital room and result in casualties.

Right now, his main focus had to be to remove the little boy from danger. As soon as he was sure Danny was safe, he'd go back and see if he couldn't catch Reed unaware and disarm him before somebody got hurt. Particularly Lindy.

Holding the child's hand, he led him down the hallway, pausing at the first desk they came to. "Is Samantha Waltham on duty today?"

The nurse at the station checked her computer and smiled. "Sure is. You'll find her in E.R."

"Thanks."

Danny resisted going farther. "I don't wanna go see her. Mama said I don't have to anymore."

"She's your mother's friend. I saw them having lunch together."

"Yeah, but..."

"No arguments," Thad said firmly.

He hated to be so stern with the boy but this was a situation that left no room for discussion. Nor was he going to be able to explain much to the nurse he sought. Hopefully, her instincts would be good enough to pick up on the urgency of his request.

They found her coming out of a cubicle and stripping off latex gloves. The moment she recognized Danny she grinned.

"Well, hello. Did you come to visit your mama? I heard she was a patient here, I just haven't had time to drop in on her yet."

Thad caught her eye and shook his head as he said, "That wouldn't be a good idea right now."

"Oh?" She arched a dark brow. "Why not?"

"Trust me, okay?" He grasped Danny's shoulders and shoved him toward the nurse. "You were his CASA worker, right? You can look after him for a few minutes?"

"I was. And I'll be glad to." Her eyes narrowed. "Care to tell me what's going on?"

"I will as soon as I can," Thad said, hoping his demeanor was a lot more placid than he felt on the inside. "Please?"

Samantha gently caressed the child's thin shoulder as she pulled him closer. "Is Lindy okay?"

Thad immediately said, "Yes," but he could tell by the way the nurse tensed that she wasn't fooled.

"You're sure you know what you're doing?"

"In this situation, yes," Thad insisted. "As long as I'm sure Danny will be safe with you."

"Of course."

About to turn and head back to Lindy's room, Thad heard shouting in the background.

Thankfully, Samantha didn't wait to see what was going on. She scooped up the child in her arms and hurried in the opposite direction.

Three burly men clad in heavy jackets and boots burst through the automatic doors and careened into the hospital lobby. They were grappling with each other and rolling around on the polished tile floor while one of the regular security guards tried unsuccessfully to break them up.

Sirens began to wail. Red-and-blue lights flashed through the glass of the E.R. doors and the other entrance that led to admitting.

Thad couldn't imagine any worse scenario, given the touchy situation in Lindy's room. If Reed got the wrong idea and thought the police had been summoned to confront him, there was no telling what he might do! Or who he might harm.

He whirled and headed back the way he had come at a run. Hospital staff members were rushing in the opposite direction, toward the sounds of trouble. So was Adelaide Crowe.

Thad reached out to try to stop her. She shook him off without pausing and tore past.

A sense of foreboding filled Thad. If Adelaide had been called away from her post before her replacement arrived, that meant there was no guard on Lindy. No one to keep her safe.

Bursting into the room, Thad first noticed that the bed was empty. His breath caught. His heart was pounding so hard he could feel his pulse in his temples.

Moments later, after he had checked every place anyone could hide, he gave a loud groan. He had failed.

Lindy was gone.

And so was James Reed.

* * *

An icy wind whipped at her hair as Lindy and Reed left the hospital. She pulled her jacket tighter and held it closed as he shepherded her to his car and ordered, "Get in."

Lindy was so frustrated she could hardly think straight, let alone hope to plot an effective escape. Her emotions mirrored the weather that morning—wildly turbulent and getting worse by the minute.

"Look," she told her captor, "it's not going to do you any good to kidnap me like this. Nobody else knows anything about the money you're looking for, either."

"Maybe you're right," he said with a sneer. "What I should have done was get my hands on your kid so you'd be more inclined to cooperate."

Eyes wide, head pounding, Lindy gaped at him. He was right. If she had been privy to Ben's secrets, there was no way she'd have stayed mute knowing Danny was in jeopardy.

"Let me be perfectly clear," she said as she labored to keep her tone even. "I do not now, nor have I ever, had any information about my late husband's business affairs. Whatever Ben did he did on his own. There is absolutely nothing you or anyone else can do to me to make me remember something I never knew in the first place."

Reed chuckled. "I'm beginning to believe you

don't realize what you actually do know. There has to be some little detail, some fact you're overlooking because you don't see it as important."

At the end of her endurance, Lindy screamed, "No! No, no, no. I don't know a thing."

"Calm down. You'll have plenty of time to sit and think where we're going." His voice lowered until it was almost a growl. "And you will *stay* there until you come up with the answers I need. No matter how long it takes."

Lindy had no rebuttal. She was sure Thad or someone else must have missed her by now, but whether or not they had found the cryptic message she'd left on the mirror was another question. And, even if they did see the toothpaste streaks, that didn't mean they'd understand what she was trying to convey.

Oh, Father, Lindy prayed, *help me. Help us all. I don't care about the money, I just want to go home to my son and to Thad.*

To Thad? she repeated to herself, already knowing that answer was *yes.* Thad was now an intrinsic part of her life and would hopefully play an even bigger part in her future. Assuming she had a future.

"I will," Lindy murmured under her breath. "I will live through this trial and I will have another chance for happiness."

She truly believed that. She had to. Visualizing a different outcome was beyond unacceptable.

Thad had immediately raced to the side entrance of the hospital and scanned the parking lot because he knew he had not passed Lindy or James Reed in the main hallway.

When he failed to see them driving away, he returned to look for Adelaide and explain to her.

"How do you know she didn't leave on her own?" the deputy demanded.

"Because Lindy wouldn't do that." Thad was adamant. "He forced her at gunpoint. I know he did."

With her own sidearm drawn, Adelaide searched Lindy's empty room. "Did you see a gun?"

"I didn't have to. Lindy told me that he was armed."

"And this Reed guy just let you waltz out of here with the boy after that?"

Thad could tell from her raised eyebrows that she didn't believe his story.

"We communicated without words. But I know exactly what she meant. Once you'd left the doorway unguarded, he was free to just march her out."

"I was following orders," Adelaide insisted. "Boyd had radioed that he was ready to relieve me just before that fight started at the other end of the hospital. I assumed he was right around the corner, so when the call came requesting backup in the lobby, I responded."

"Only Boyd did, too?"

"Yeah." She pulled a face and holstered her weapon. Thad saw her pausing to look in the mirror over the bathroom sink. At first he thought she was checking her own appearance. Then, she said, "C'mere a sec."

"What?"

The deputy pointed. "Does this mean anything to you?"

Thad squinted at the bluish smears. "That looks like the letter *P,* twice. It could mean Pearson Products."

"What about this little figure of a man down here? Any idea what that's supposed to be for?"

Studying the crude drawing, Thad was struck by the notion that it looked less like a person than it did an airplane. Those two things fit together perfectly. His business bordered the Serenity airport. If Lindy had wanted to leave behind a picture clue, choosing a plane made more sense than trying to draw an obscure kitchen tool.

Whirling, he headed for the doorway.

"Hold it. The sheriff will want to talk to you," the deputy called after him.

Thad ignored her. He knew exactly where he needed to go and nobody was going to delay him.

Not now. Not when Lindy's very life might hang in the balance.

Behind him, he heard Adelaide starting to shout. Judging by what she was saying, he figured she was radioing other officers to cut him off and detain him.

That was not going to happen. He was on a mission. A rescue mission. Probably one of the most important of his entire career.

He straight-armed the side door, leaned into the increasing wind for balance and raced toward his truck. Thankfully, there had been no empty places close by and he'd had to park out on the fringe, away from the main buildings.

Sliding behind the wheel he gunned the engine, dropped the pickup in gear and heard its tires whine as they spun in the loose gravel.

"Quiet. Don't attract attention," he muttered to himself, easing up and pulling out into the road. The cops would probably be right behind him, particularly if Adelaide mentioned what they'd discussed about Lindy's message.

That was all right with Thad. It might be advantageous to have some backup, especially if they ended up in a shoot-out with Reed or some of his cronies.

Remembering the noisy altercation in the hospital, Thad decided it must have been staged to cover Reed's escape. That figured. A guy who was desperate enough to come after Lindy with a gun was probably willing to try almost anything, including enlisting the help of others. The man had used fall guys before and there was no reason to assume he'd changed his methods since.

The truck slid around a tight corner. Some of the toys that Danny had insisted on bringing along slipped off the seat onto the floor and landed with a plastic-sounding rattle and crash.

Thad disregarded the mess. If the stuff was broken he'd buy new toys to replace them. He had far more crucial problems at the moment than whether or not the boy's personal possessions had been damaged.

Out of the corner of his eye, he noted a couple of robot-looking things, an electronic handheld game and the little computer Danny often used for more complicated entertainment. The kid's hand-eye coordination was already nearly as good as some of the operators who'd handled drones in combat and Thad realized he was as proud of the boy as if he were his own son.

Could their relationship someday become that? he wondered absently. Were the doctors ever going to tell him it was safe for him to think of starting a family, beginning with making Lindy his wife?

That thought was so heartrending it hurt. His hands fisted on the wheel. He had meant it when he'd tried to let her know he loved her and although she hadn't responded in kind, he wanted to think she would have under other circumstances.

What he needed to do now was provide the chance for her to admit she loved him, too. And to do that, he had to free her from her captor without endangering her well-being any more than it already was.

If this had been a combat situation he would have known exactly what to do. He would have had snipers waiting to pick off Reed the instant he dared show his face.

And now? Thad asked himself.

Now, all the advantages were on the side of their enemy. He would not only have to face Reed solo, he would have to do it empty-handed.

But he would triumph. He had to. Lindy's life depended upon him, and him alone.

SIXTEEN

Lindy didn't want to have anything to do with James Reed, let alone converse with him. However, as they drove toward the airport in his black sedan, a few elements of her dilemma puzzled her enough to trigger questions.

Licking her parched lips and fighting to appear normal when she was actually scared to death, she asked, "What about all those letters?"

"What letters?" His head snapped around.

"The ones in Ben's handwriting. You kept leaving them where I could find them."

His thick eyebrows knit. "I don't know what you're talking about. I don't have anything Ben wrote. What did these letters look like?"

"They were scribbled messages on his letterhead. Old ones, obviously. But they all mentioned money so I figured they came from you."

"Not from me." The frown deepened. "I suppose the criminals Ben got mixed up with could have saved them. Who were they addressed to?"

"Nobody. They were more like a shopping list or a memo. You know. Informal."

"Interesting."

Lindy actually believed his denial. "Okay. If you weren't responsible for the messages, then who was?"

"I wish I knew." His glance kept darting from the road ahead to the side and rear mirrors as if he expected to spot the police on his trail any second.

"Care to guess?"

Reed huffed. "It beats me. Considering all the different people who know about Ben's secret, it could be almost anybody."

"Such as?" The way Lindy saw her situation, the more facts she had to work with, the more likely she'd be able to triumph. Eventually.

Punctuating his answer with muttered cursing, Reed finally said, "I came into this mess late, okay? I had no idea that your dear departed husband was dirty, not until the drug cops started poking around the office and asking questions. At that time, I figured I was doing well to keep my own neck out of the noose."

"So, what changed?"

"I told you. I found out about the secret accounts Ben had established for skimming a bigger cut for himself. I really did start out by hoping to earn a finder's fee. But then I got to thinking. Why shouldn't I have it all?"

"You mean to tell me that the men you hired to ransack my house weren't from Ben's past?"

"Ransack? All I did was pay a couple guys to break in and hack your computer so I could have a copy of all your files."

Totally confused, Lindy rubbed her temples where a headache had already taken hold. "Then you gave that information to the DEA? Why?"

"To prove I was on the side of law and order and collect a finder's fee." Reed chuckled wryly. "And because I couldn't find what I was looking for and wanted to see if they could." His humor waned. "I told them I'd stumbled on that info in Ben's files, but it didn't help. They apparently didn't have any better luck than I did."

"Duh! That's because there was nothing to find," she insisted. "When is everybody going to figure that out?"

Although he didn't reply for several minutes, Lindy could tell that her captor was considering her conclusion. There was no way she could make anybody believe her, of course, because it was impossible to prove a negative. In a way, she wished she did have something to reveal so everyone would leave her alone.

Sighing, she sank back against the plush leather seat of the car. That was when it dawned on her that he couldn't have driven to Serenity and also have flown.

"Wait a second. If you flew up from Little Rock, how did your car get here?"

"I drove. My pilot followed with the plane."

Terrific. Now she had two men to worry about eluding.

"You'll never get away with this, you know," Lindy told him. "Thad knows you were in my room and so does the deputy you had to pass to deliver the flowers. Plus, when you abandon this car at the airport, they'll be sure it was really you."

He cackled. "I love the way your devious mind works. Haven't you figured it out yet? I don't care who knows I was involved. You and I will be out of U.S. jurisdiction long before anybody comes after us."

"Wait a second. You can't take me out of the country. I don't even have a passport."

That triggered genuine laughter and rankled her all the way to the soles of her sneakers. He thought ruining her life was *funny?* Well, she sure didn't.

The more she contemplated the developing situation the madder she got. This was more than unfair—it was totally unacceptable.

"I am not going to get in any airplane with you," Lindy vowed. "I'm no good to you dead so you won't shoot me."

"No, but I can tie you up and load you like baggage," Reed countered. "Now shut up and let me think."

Lindy continued to monitor his changing expressions. If he'd had everything well planned out, he wouldn't need to do more thinking. Therefore, he had to be making this up as he went along, at least in part. That was a good sign.

Now, all she had to do was figure out how to take advantage of it.

The black sedan slued around the final corner and headed for the airstrip. A red-and-white twin-engine plane waited the tarmac. It was bigger than she'd expected and looked fast and sleek enough to carry them across the Gulf of Mexico as Reed had promised. Her chances of escape were looking slimmer and slimmer.

She made him literally drag her from the car, then threw her full weight against his pull as the increasingly strong wind blew her hair wildly and made the edges of her jacket flap.

Her resistance slowed his pace but didn't stop it. A man in a tan jumpsuit climbed out of the plane and came to Reed's aid by taking hold of her free arm.

"You ready?" Reed shouted over her head.

"The weather's getting worse pretty fast, sir. I think we should abort the flight."

"We're going. Period." He gestured with the gun. "You got that?"

"Yes, sir."

Continuing to struggle, Lindy would have

screamed if she'd thought it would help but, as
Danny had reminded her, it was Saturday. Nobody
was working in the warehouse today and no one
lived nearby enough to hear her. There was no use
wasting her breath.

The loud roar of a motor and the squeal of sliding tires drew everyone's attention.

The men who had been tugging Lindy along
froze.

Seeing the approach of Thad's old, blue truck,
she wasn't sure whether to be glad he'd come or
to wish he'd stayed away for his own safety. Even
if he happened to be armed, which she doubted,
one against two was hardly a fair fight.

She flipped her wind-whipped hair out of her
eyes with a toss of her head so she could watch.

Thad's truck skidded to a stop, and through the
windshield she saw him lean over for a second,
then straighten.

She was holding her breath and trembling when
he opened the driver's-side door and stepped out.

Choosing to grab the child's netbook off the
floor of his truck and use it as a decoy had been
an afterthought.

Thad didn't know if his ruse would work. At
that point, he was so low on options he figured
anything was worth a try.

With his hands raised, he waved the one containing the small, portable computer. It had hit the floor when all the toys had slid off the seat. He sure hoped the cracking sound he'd heard had come from some other source because if this device wasn't working enough to at least display a picture, he was toast.

"Stay where you are," Reed shouted above the rising roar of the wind. "Don't try to stop us."

Thad shrugged and paused. "Fine with me. If you don't want the keys to Ben's offshore accounts, that's not my problem."

"What are you talking about?"

Thad gave another wave with the rectangular object. "This. We all overlooked it."

"What is it?"

"Danny's games. What better place to hide something than in plain sight?"

He saw Lindy's jaw drop and hoped she would have sense enough to play along.

"Bring it over here," Reed ordered.

"Let her go first."

"Not on your life. Not until I see that you're telling the truth."

"Hey, I'm no computer expert. I'm just the delivery guy."

"Then how do you know the account numbers are on there?"

"They have to be. Think about it. Southerland was smart enough to skim from drug gangs, launder their money through a hedge fund and hide a fortune from everybody, even the feds. Where would you stash those numbers if you were him, especially if you thought you might be killed?" He spared a quick glance for Lindy and added, "Sorry."

"I'll need proof."

Thad had anticipated that reaction. Reed was no fool. If anything foiled him, it would be his monumental greed.

"The computer, and me, in trade for the woman," Thad shouted. "You'd better hurry and make up your mind. The cops are on my tail. They'll be here soon."

Instead of complying, the businessman pressed a pistol against Lindy's temple and smiled. "All right. We'll hurry. Get over here before I end this standoff the messy way."

Thad wasn't about to let him harm Lindy.

He came forward.

His best hope was that Reed would be unable to access the files on the boy's game player and would delay taking any overt action until he had contacted his own expert.

While there was life, there was a chance.

And while there was prayer, there was hope.

Lindy could not believe anyone could be as brave as Thad Pearson. Not only had he come after her, he was offering to become a part of the situation that might very well lead to their demise. If she'd had any lingering doubts about his love, they were long gone.

And her own tender feelings? Those were just as clear. She loved Thad so much, so fully, she would have walked barefoot across a bed of hot coals to save him, if need be.

As he drew closer and their eyes met, she tried to read his thoughts, to tell if he was being truthful about Danny's computer notebook. The notion was just far-fetched enough to be true yet crazy enough to possibly be nothing more than a figment of Thad's imagination.

The hardest thing for Lindy to accept was that he was there with her. She knew she shouldn't be glad to see him. Part of her heart was rejoicing while another part wept. They could not die. Not now. Not when she had just admitted how much they belonged together.

And poor Danny. He couldn't lose them both. *Please, God, protect us.*

Stepping behind Lindy, James Reed gestured with the gun. "Into the plane. Pearson first."

The pilot had already climbed aboard and was checking his instruments.

When Thad passed Lindy she could tell how badly he felt that he hadn't been able to get her freed so she managed a smile for his benefit and whispered, "Thank you for trying."

Reed gave her arm a shake. "Shut up. Now you And don't try anything stupid. We won't be flying high enough to need cabin pressure so I won' hesitate to shoot."

Lindy slid into a seat directly across the narrow aisle from Thad and fumbled to fasten he seat belt. The pilot was at the controls of the plan and Reed positioned himself to the rear, behin them all.

Powerful engines coughed to life, one at a time making it hard to hear normal conversational tone above their rumble.

"Get started finding those numbers," Reed shouted. He gestured with the barrel of his pisto

"I told you, I'm no expert," Thad protested.

"That's not what your service record says."

Lindy chanced a peek at her seatmate and saw his jaw muscles clenching. Their nemesis had don his homework. Perhaps that was why he had be lieved Thad's wild claim in the first place.

Wondering how long Thad could stall and how soon Reed was going to lose patience and elimi nate him, Lindy closed her eyes and began to pra silently while tears trickled down her cheeks.

There were no flowery words to her prayer, jus a heartfelt plea for deliverance.

The hardest part was remaining hopeful in spite of what was happening all around her.

Rolling down the runway and gaining speed, the Cessna was buffeted and shaken by the wind.

As she felt the wheels of the plane finally break contact with the ground, her spirits sank like a stone in a bottomless well.

Thad began by powering up the unit and fiddling with the games as if he were actually searching the internal database. He knew Reed was watching him closely but he could also tell that the man was essentially clueless when it came to computers. That was good to know, although it probably also meant that his patience would soon wear thin.

Rising above the treetops, the plane banked hard to the left, enabling Thad to see the town passing below. They were going west, at least at the moment, although their ultimate destination was anybody's guess. This particular aircraft had a pretty decent range so they could be headed anywhere, especially if they stopped for gas to top off the wing tanks.

Below, Thad spotted rows of cars with flashing red-and-blue lights speeding toward Pearson Products, undoubtedly pursuing him. Too bad they hadn't been a little faster acting on the cryptic clues Lindy had left on the hospital mirror.

Thad thought it would raise her spirits if he complimented her intelligence so he smiled over at her and said, "I'm glad you brushed your teeth this morning."

She perked up and sniffled. "Thanks." Sobering, she swiped away sparse tears. "I almost wish I hadn't."

"It was the smart thing to do," Thad assured her.

"Knock off the flirting," Reed ordered. "How are you coming with those files?"

"It's slow. If he's embedded anything in these programs, it'll take a while to find the back door. Maybe even days. Weeks."

"You have exactly half an hour." He was waving the gun wildly and appeared close to losing control of himself. "After that, I start shooting. I just haven't decided which one of you to kill first."

Half an hour? The man had to be even crazier than he'd first thought.

Thad peeked over at Lindy and saw her trying to smile back at him. If he managed to fake some banking or routing numbers, it might delay their deaths for a little while but that wasn't good enough. He'd also have to disarm the gunman without drawing fire from the pilot or risking Lindy's safety. It would be a lot easier to predict the outcome of their touchy situation if he didn't have to look out for anyone besides himself.

Fingers absently tapping the keyboard, Thad

opened the program files and found the parental control security function. This little laptop had a surprising 160 GB hard drive and an Intel processor, proving that it was even more capable of hiding files than he'd imagined.

He glanced over at Lindy. "Do you have any idea what password Ben might have used to lock Danny out?"

"No. Sorry."

"Mother's maiden name, a dog he once had? Anything like that?"

Lindy shook her head. "Ben would have been a lot more likely to have used something technical. Maybe a series of numbers?"

"It might take forever to figure that out," Thad replied. "I'll try a few random words first."

Success came on his third try. The password was "retirement." Ironic, in a way, since Ben had been permanently retired from life, itself, by his involvement with criminals.

Watching—leaning over the back of Thad's seat and bracing himself by hanging on with his free hand—Reed shouted, "That's it! You did it."

"I got into the parental controls," Thad told him. "That doesn't mean I'm going to be able to find anything else."

"You'd better."

The plane was being rocked so badly by this time it felt as if they were sitting on the ground in the middle of a massive earthquake. They'd climb a bit, then stutter or abruptly lose altitude as if all the lift had disappeared from beneath their wings

Thad could tell that their captor was having trouble staying in his own seat because the gun was waving around and he was holding on with his free hand—meaning he hadn't fastened his safety belt.

"Why don't you play it safe and buckle up?" Thad suggested. "I'll let you know what else I find."

Reed's laugh was cynical and harsh. "No way I'm staying right here where I can watch you."

"Suit yourself. Feels to me like this weather is getting worse by the second."

The pilot agreed with a shout. "I can pull us out of some of this turbulence if I climb to a higher altitude, Mr. Reed."

"No! Stay under the radar the way I told you. How far are we from Lake Norfork?"

"Five or ten minutes. We've got a terrible head-wind."

Thad's survival instincts were firing on all cylinders. Wanting to know when they were over the lake might mean that Reed had something specific in mind. No matter what it was, it couldn't be good news for his prisoners.

Paging down the list of files he had accessed, Thad wasn't really looking for banking information. He was simply searching on autopilot while stalling for time and wondering if he dared make a grab for the moving gun barrel during the next big lurch of the plane.

Something on the screen caught his eye. He froze with his index finger poised. *Whoa! Could it be? Was his ruse actually going to pan out?*

Staring in disbelief, he suddenly realized that Ben Southerland had done exactly what Thad had been pretending he'd done. The secret files *were* on the child's computer. And he had just located them.

Now what? If he dared let on that he'd been successful, Reed would surely shoot him and probably get rid of Lindy, too, rather than leave witnesses behind.

Glancing over at her, he saw that she was staring at the computer screen.

Although the nod of his head was barely perceptible, Thad knew she had seen his signal. Her eyes widened. Her lips parted.

"I need to use the restroom," she said abruptly.

Reed snorted. "This is a little plane, not a commercial flight, lady. We don't have all the amenities on board. You're out of luck."

"Then can I at least stretch my legs a bit?"

"And get behind me? I don't think so." He called to the pilot. "Frank. Circle over the lake. I'm about to lose patience with our passengers and one of them is going to be getting off if he doesn't start to make some progress soon."

Thad realized his time was running out. He began to grin as he held up the little device and pointed. "I'm there. Here's your precious file."

It didn't come as a surprise to Thad when the man got excited but he was taken aback when he leaned closer to get a better look.

That was all the opening Thad needed.

He closed his fist around the man's wrist and yanked. When Reed's head and shoulders lurched forward, Thad's other fist connected with his chin.

That blow threw the businessman off balance. Recoiling and falling backward, he squeezed off one wild shot before hitting his head and falling unconscious.

Lindy had already ducked as low in her seat as the lap belt would allow. The bullet passed her, ricocheted off a cabinet in the cockpit and clipped the pilot in the temple.

He didn't shout or even moan. He simply slumped over the controls.

The weight of his body against the yoke dropped the nose of the plane. Already flying low, they began to descend rapidly.

Thad saw icy-cold Lake Norfork looming ahead. The wind had whipped the surface and created the kind of whitecaps usually reserved for the ocean. Those waves would make their land-

ng even rougher, maybe even causing the plane
o break up on impact!

He shouted, "Brace yourself! Cover your head,"
s he unfastened his lap belt and launched himself
oward the unconscious pilot.

Grabbing his shoulders, Thad shoved back his
ody and took hold of the yoke, hoping to muscle
he plane out of its lethal dive.

The aircraft shuddered, straining to survive.
Vhen they had started to descend, their air speed
ad risen.

Thad saw the water coming. Fast. Unforgiving.

They were going to ditch.

There was nothing he could do to stop it.

SEVENTEEN

Lindy's prayers were wordless. Constant. Frantic.

She could feel the angle of the cabin floor beginning to change beneath her feet. G-forces pressed her back against her seat as the plane leveled out.

Then, just as she started to raise her head to look, one wing dipped, caught in the rough water and made the aircraft spin on that axis. Moments later there was a terrific jolt when everything came to an abrupt halt.

Lindy felt as if a giant hand had reached up and slammed her against the seat. The lap belt dug into her thighs. She hurt so badly she cried out.

The noise and impact of the collision seemed to go on for countless minutes before the forward momentum ebbed.

Surrounded by silence, Lindy sensed a different kind of pitching, as if they were being gently rocked.

That has to be the movement of the waves, she

reasoned, half conscious and wondering if she was the only one who realized they had crashed.

She pushed herself upright and blinked, hardly able to take it all in. They were down, all right. The plane's nose was partially submerged and water had begun to seep into the passenger compartment, although the wings seemed to be acting as temporary flotation devices.

Her mind began to shriek, *Get out!*

The belt holding her was so taut it was binding and stopping the quick-release from working. She clawed at it until the tips of her nails broke. Tears of frustration and terror further blurred her vision.

When a masculine and very familiar voice said, "Take it easy. I'll get that for you," she nearly shrieked with joy in spite of everything.

"Thad! Are you okay?"

"Better than the other two guys."

"Are—are they dead?"

"No. The pilot is wounded and Reed is out like a light but they're both still breathing."

His brute strength forced the clasp of her seat belt to finally let loose and she sensed that he was lifting her, so she wrapped her arms around his neck.

"Tell me you can swim. Please," he said, sounding short of breath.

"I can. Can you?"

"Yeah. Don't worry about me. Just swim free of the plane and head for the nearest shoreline."

"But…"

"No arguments, Lindy. Not this time. If this thing sinks, it's liable to create a suction that drags you down with it. The farther away you are, the safer you'll be."

He had to kick the side door to get it to open and a gust of wind nearly tore it from its hinges.

Placing her on her feet in the opening, he pointed to the shore. "It's not that far. Get going."

"What about you? Aren't you coming with me?"

"I'll be out soon. I want to see if I can help the pilot first."

"What about Reed? Where's his gun?"

"I have it," Thad said, pointing to the dark metal grip sticking out of his belt. "He can't hurt us anymore."

"I don't want to leave you," she insisted. "I—I…"

Say it. Tell him you love him. Now. Before it's too late.

Lindy steeled herself against the possibility that this might be the very last time she and Thad spoke.

Before she could follow her heart and confess that she shared his feelings, he put the flat of his hand between her shoulder blades and gave her a mighty shove.

Plummeting feetfirst into the icy, turbulent

water stole Lindy's breath away. She gasped, taking in more than air, and bobbed to the surface coughing and gagging. If anyone but Thad had pushed her like that, she'd have been furious.

"Go. Swim!" he shouted at her with one hand cupped around his mouth and the other arm pressed against his side as if babying his ribs. "Do it now."

She was trembling all the way to the marrow of her bones, so cold she wondered if she was able to make the swim. She had to try. Thad had already risked his life for her sake more than once and was now trying to save others. She couldn't disappoint him.

What Lindy wanted most to do was tread water long enough to give him a piece of her mind. Only the knowledge that he was right about putting distance between herself and the sinking aircraft and the realization that she had her son's future to consider made her kick off her shoes, turn and strike out for shore.

Movement became instinctive as she fell into a rhythm. Kick. Stroke. Breathe.

And silently weep for the loneliness she could already envision if Thad Pearson went down with that plane.

Thad gritted his teeth against the stabbing pain in his side and struggled to reach the pilot once again. A name he'd overheard popped into his head so he tried it. "Frank? Frank! Wake up. We need to get out of here."

The man stirred, then tensed as if he thought he was under attack.

Thad dodged a weak, ineffectual punch and smiled. "I see you're awake. Suppose you help me get your boss up and move him out onto the wing. I don't think I can do it alone."

"What happened?" Frank was testing his temple. His fingers came away bloody.

"Reed shot you."

"No way."

"Suit yourself," Thad said. "If you want to sit there and argue with me, fine. I'm getting out of here before she sinks."

The pilot staggered slightly as he stood but quickly widened his stance and regained his balance.

In view of the increasingly tilting floor, Thad figured they'd be doing well to get themselves and Reed outside in time.

The businessman's body wasn't large but it was dead-weight. Frank looped his arms under his boss's while Thad grabbed Reed's ankles.

By this time, anything that had been knocked loose by the crash was bobbing or submerged in the aisle so the rescuers had to shuffle their feet to keep from tripping.

"Where's the girl?" Frank shouted, sounding genuinely concerned.

"Already out and on her way to shore," Thad answered.

"Good. Just for the record, I had no idea what this idiot had planned. I'd never have gone along with it if I had."

"Why didn't you refuse to take off from Serenity then?"

"Because I wasn't keen on being shot. He could have flown himself if he'd had to. He has a pilot's license. He made it clear he didn't need me nearly as much as I wanted to come out of this alive."

"Understood."

Thad's foot slipped on something flat and slightly raised as he reached the exit. It wasn't until he'd helped the others out onto the wing that he realized it might have been Danny's computer.

Did he care? Nope. Not enough to risk survival by going back. Money was highly overrated when judged against a man's life.

The pilot dropped Reed's shoulders onto the wing and straightened, leaning into the gusting wind for balance. "Look! There's a boat on its way."

Thad was about to cheer when he realized their erstwhile rescuers might inadvertently run right over Lindy!

Where was she? He couldn't see anyone in the water from where he was standing.

Thad began to jump up and down, mindless of the shooting pain his ribs, waving and shouting. "Look out!"

The pitch of the small boat's engine changed as the craft accelerated. Its wake rose, sending twin rooster tails high on both sides. Even if those boaters didn't manage to catch Lindy in their propeller wash there was a chance that a rough wake would be enough to cause her to falter and drown.

Thad realized what he had to do.

He took as deep a breath as his injury would permit, dived into the frigid waves and struck out in the direction he'd told Lindy to swim.

Right then, he wasn't sure whether to pray that she had actually followed his orders or hope that she hadn't.

Lindy was so cold she could hardly draw enough breath to keep her going. Above the whistling wind she could hear the plane making ominous, bubbling sounds.

Treading water, she looked back. One intact wing was still afloat but the other, plus the plane's nose and part of the passenger compartment, was slipping beneath the rough surface.

Her tears mixed with the lake water dripping from her face, her hair. There was no sign of Thad.

And it looked as if the small Cessna was about to sink.

Suddenly, she heard a roar. At first she thought it was nothing more than the sound of the approaching storm. Then she realized she was hearing a motorboat. Was rescue on the way?

Lightning flashed in the distance. The already turbulent surface of the enormous lake began to show expanding circles as raindrops hit. In moments, the drops were pelting her hard enough to hurt and she realized there were tiny pellets of hail hidden in the precipitation.

Irony rose to temporarily strengthen her. *Next thing there'll be a meteorite streaking through the atmosphere to hit me right between the eyes!* she thought cynically. At this moment, it was hard to imagine a scenario much worse than what had already taken place.

Especially since Thad is missing, she added, feeling so bereft she could hardly breathe, hardly think.

The darkness of the storm had turned day to night. Lindy's arms ached. Her legs and feet were numb.

Drifting, she pictured her little boy, so innocent, so forlorn, particularly right after he'd lost his daddy. Poor baby. What would happen to him now? It was all well and good to have an organization like CASA looking after Danny's welfare, but what would eventually become of him if both his parents were gone?

The sky lit as jagged streaks of electricity shot between the black clouds. Thunder rumbled. Noise increased. So did the roar of the approaching boat.

Where were they? Could they see her? How could she hope to signal to them to pick her up when she had barely enough strength left to lift an arm, let alone shout?

Closing her eyes in spite of willing herself to remain alert, Lindy laid her weary head back and tried to float. To rest for just a few moments.

She didn't realize she had slipped gently beneath the waves until a strong arm closed around her and she felt herself being propelled upward.

Toward air. Toward life.

Thad's head broke the surface an instant after Lindy's. He gulped to fill his lungs and realized that the icy water had numbed his injury enough to actually help him cope.

"Breathe," he shouted, kicking to stay afloat while he shook her shoulders. "Breathe, Lindy, breathe!"

Choking had never sounded better to him. Continuing to support her, he raised his free arm and hailed the passing boat.

Whoever had been piloting the craft was

traveling too fast to stop so he steered the inboard in a tight circle and brought it to an idle beside the swimmers.

"Take the woman first," Thad ordered the second man in the boat as he pushed her toward him. "She's in shock."

"No wonder," the slicker-clad fisherman replied. "What on earth were you folks thinkin' by flyin' around in this kind of weather?"

"It's a long story," Thad managed to say.

Waiting until Lindy was safely aboard, he then accepted the man's help and collapsed onto the floor of the small boat.

"Blankets. For the woman," used up all the breath Thad had left.

The rescuer who wasn't wrestling the helm removed his slicker and draped it around Lindy's shoulders before tucking her into a niche next to the open-air wheelhouse. "Best I can do for now. We'll get you folks back to shore in a jiffy. Ambulance is on its way. My missus called 9–1–1 when she saw you hit the water. Good thing me and Dad were close to the dock."

Thad pushed himself onto one elbow and wrapped an arm around his torso to stifle the ache that was returning. "Two more. Still out there," he gasped hoarsely.

"Don't look good from here," the older man

said, stretching to peer into the distance. His adult son agreed with a nod.

Lightning flashed again, illuminating what was left of the plane.

"On the wing," Thad said. "Look on the wing."

"I see 'em."

"Both of them?"

The younger man answered. "Yeah. They're standin' up. Looks to me like they're fightin'."

"Can you get to them?"

"I'd hate to try. It looks pretty dangerous."

Ducking his head beneath the cowling for a little protection, the younger man pulled out a cell phone and used it before turning back to Thad.

"There's another boat on its way to your friends."

"Call them back and tell them to be careful," Lindy said, barely speaking above a whisper. "Those other men are criminals."

The sweet sound of her voice lifted Thad's spirits so high he experienced an influx of energy. It was enough to enable him to crawl over, join her and wrap her in his embrace.

She lifted her face to gaze at him.

Leaning closer, he pressed a kiss to her trembling lips and sighed in thanksgiving.

That was all the prayer he could manage.

He knew it was enough for the loving God who had brought them through in spite of the evil that had tried so hard to destroy them.

* * *

Lindy rested her head on Thad's shoulder and let the tears fall. They had survived. They were still alive, still together.

A guttural shout from the older rescuer jolted her from her reverie.

"Looks like she's sinkin'. Other boat's gonna be too late," he yelled. "I'm goin' in."

The engine roared and the bow rose. Centrifugal force pushed her harder against Thad while contact with the waves and pouring rain battered the small craft and made it buck like a wild bronco.

Lindy heard Thad stifle a moan. "Are you hurt?"

"Just a couple of cracked ribs, I think," he replied. "I'll be fine."

"Thank goodness. I was afraid he'd shot you."

"No. If he'd been a better fighter, he might have had a chance but I disarmed him easily." He managed a wry chuckle. "If I'd let a wimpy businessman get the better of me, I'd never live it down with my marine buddies."

Thad gave her a quick kiss on the temple, then pivoted onto his knees and wiped water from his face so he could better observe what lay ahead.

Not to be outdone, Lindy mimicked his pose. What she saw was so alarming she gasped. The forward section of the plane was nearly submerged. One wing now rose in the air while the other, the one that had been damaged during landing, was no longer visible.

"The weight of the twin engines will probably tip it forward," Thad shouted. "When it goes under, it'll be like letting the water out of a bathtub. Anything too close will get sucked down, too."

"I know," the fisherman at the wheel yelled back. "I'll hold off a safe distance. See if you can get those fellas to listen to you and swim toward us. It's their best chance."

"I'll try." Thad cupped his hands around his mouth and shouted, "Frank! Swim for it. You're running out of time."

The shadowy figures standing on the wing parted. One of them dived off the highest point and started to stroke through the water as powerfully as if he were training for the Olympics.

"Reed. You, too," Thad hollered. "We'll pick you up."

At first, it looked to Lindy as though James Reed was going to accept their offer. Then he turned, jumped feetfirst into the lake next to the open doorway, and disappeared.

"What's he doing?" the younger fisherman asked.

"I think he's just crazy enough to go back after the key to the treasure he's been chasing for so long," Lindy said, shaking her head. She looked to Thad. "Do you think he'll make it?"

"I don't know."

Watching the red-and-white fuselage shifting, she gasped. The top of the doorway was sliding underwater. Even if Reed did manage to reach Danny's computer, was he going to be able to exit with it in time to save himself?

The tail section rose, hanging almost motionless for several seconds that seemed to stretch endlessly. Then, as if gliding along a perfectly smooth pathway, it disappeared beneath the wind-whipped surface.

Lightning flashed. Lindy peered through the rain, straining to see if there was a man bobbing in the water where the plane had been.

Only bubbles marked the spot. There was no sign of Reed. "He's gone, isn't he?"

"I think so." Thad's arm tightened around her shoulders.

The boat circled, engine idling, and Lindy watched Thad help the fishermen pull in the pilot over the side.

"He was..." Frank said between coughs and gasps, "a greedy fool. I told him he'd never make it."

"He went back for the computer?" Thad asked.

"Yeah. Said he wasn't going to let it go." Frank paused for another coughing fit. "Guess he didn't."

"Maybe he figured we'd turn him in to the police," Lindy said. "I wish we could."

"So do I," Thad agreed. "But at least we know what was going on."

Lindy tugged on his hand and urged him to join her beneath the only shelter, the tiny niche in the bow next to the wheel.

Once they were settled, she slipped her arms around Thad's waist, closed her eyes and held him gently.

She had never been colder.

She had never been wetter.

And she had never, ever, imagined that she could be this happy.

EPILOGUE

Once Harlan Allgood, Chief Kelso and supervisors from the DEA had compared notes, they concluded that Lindy had been the victim of greed on several fronts. James Reed had been the catalyst that had brought it all to a head.

She was having coffee in the sheriff's office with the sheriff and Thad, while Harlan explained more fully. Danny cuddled close and sipped a cup of hot chocolate.

"The agents who misused their power have been reprimanded and demoted," the portly sheriff said. "They falsified the bank records, ruined your credit, and that got you evicted. I suspect they planted the drugs in the house, too, but we can't prove it. They keep insisting it must have been Ben's old associates who did that. They figured in all this, too."

"Everybody was after the same thing? Ben's hidden money?" Lindy asked.

"Yeah." Harlan looked to Thad. "I thought you might be involved, too, for a while there."

Smiling, the ex-marine nodded. "I was involved, all right, only I was on Lindy's side." He set aside his coffee mug and reached for her hand. "Still am."

"Good for you." The sheriff chortled. "Just see that you don't so much as get a speeding ticket in this town. Adelaide is still mad enough to throw you in jail for any little misstep."

"Sorry about that." Thad gave Lindy's hand an affectionate squeeze. "I'm still confused about the break-ins. They weren't all done by the same people?"

"No. Reed sent the guys who copied Miz Southerland's computer records. The ones who smashed into her car, left the notes and planted that nasty dead critter were from Ben's former life. When we arrested them they admitted they'd heard about the money, too, and wanted to see if they could turn up anything or spook her into going after it."

Smiling slightly, Lindy breathed a noisy sigh. "They had no idea how close they were when they trashed poor Danny's room." Her smile grew more wistful and she hugged the child on her lap. "I can't believe it's finally all over. I don't know how I can ever thank you. Both of you."

Thad and the sheriff exchanged knowing glances before Harlan pushed back his chair and got to his feet. "Now that all your belongings have been moved back into your house, compliments of those yahoos who faked your loan default, you can thank me by not suing my department for false arrest."

"I wouldn't dream of suing," Lindy said amiably, noting his look of relief before he ambled away.

She felt Thad touch her hand as soon as the three of them were alone.

"And you can thank *me* by continuing to make my office run smoothly," he said. "You know how desperately I need a good executive assistant." He smiled at Danny. "And a helper."

Lindy had not expected such a businesslike approach. Not after their joint brush with death and his confession of love in her hospital room.

She'd thought she was masking her disappointment fairly well until Thad began to chuckle.

Her brows arched. "What's so funny?"

"*You* are," he said with compassion that made her shiver and sent her pulse through the roof. "What I should have said was, I need a partner. For life."

Speechless, Lindy simply stared at him.

Her son, however, had no problem finding something to say.

"Can we, Mama? Can we be partners?"

Eyes wide, Lindy hushed the boy. "I don't think that's exactly what Mr. Pearson meant, honey."

"She's right," Thad explained. "As soon as my doctors say I'm well enough, I'd like to marry your mother. How does that sound?"

The child hooted as though he'd been presented with the perfect gift. "All right!"

Lindy was grinning so widely her cheeks hurt. "I'm so glad you approve."

Sobering, Thad asked, "Do *you* approve? We might not have much money, but I promise I'll do my best to make you happy. Both of you."

She caressed his cheek, gazing into his eyes. "We'll have everything we need. We'll be a family. Yes, yes, yes. I can't wait to become your wife."

At that moment, the sheriff poked his head back through the doorway, cleared his throat and chuckled. "'Scuse me, folks. I hate to interrupt but I thought you might like to know that a team of divers located your kid's computer in the lake. You two are gonna get a reward that'd choke a horse. Thought y'all might like to know, in case you were makin' plans for the future or something."

As Harlan eased the door closed again, Lindy turned to the man she loved so much it was beyond comprehension. "You were saying?"

Thad's smile lifted one corner of his mouth higher than the other and his eyes twinkled mischievously. "I don't remember. Was it important?"

Laughing lightly and wondering if it was possible to be any happier, Lindy landed a playful blow on his shoulder and said, "Part of it certainly was."

"We're gonna get *married!*" Danny said, regarding the adults as if they were both acting ridiculous.

"Oh, that. Yeah, I guess I do recall mentioning that." Thad was gazing tenderly at Lindy as he pulled her into his arms. "Maybe you'd better do something to keep me from forgetting again."

Lindy made a contented sound and lifted her face to accept his kiss. This was one experience she was certainly *never* going to forget.

And judging by his loud cheering and jumping up and down, neither was her little boy.

* * * * *

Dear Reader,

This is the third book for The Defenders and will hopefully not be the last. I have other commitments to fulfill before I can write more about CASA, though, so we'll all have to wait and see—me, included.

Post-traumatic stress disorder may not be as easy to overcome in real life as I have portrayed it on these pages. If you know someone who is suffering from PTSD, please don't assume that they will find such quick healing, although I pray that many will. My heart breaks for the men and women in our armed services who daily lay their lives on the line for the rest of us and who suffer so deeply, even if they come home physically uninjured. If you see people in uniform or meet veterans, shake their hands and thank them. I do that as often as possible.

If you want to write to me, email will bring the fastest reply: val@valeriehansen.com. If you would rather write a letter, my address is P.O. Box 13, Glencoe, AR 72539. There are book excerpts and other interesting info on www.valeriehansen.com.

Blessings,

Valerie Hansen

Questions for Discussion

1. Lindy is very wary of everyone when this story begins. Can you understand why she would emotionally withdraw like that after seeing her husband killed?

2. When Thad Pearson is introduced to Lindy, he is still coming to terms with unexpected changes in his plans for his future. Do you feel bad if things don't go just as you think they should? Is that productive?

3. Lindy is focused on her child above everything else, including her own happiness. Is that wise? Will it be good for Danny?

4. Lindy keeps telling herself that she is better off single. Have you ever made up your mind about something and then wondered later if you might be wrong?

5. Hackers steal Lindy's computer files and ruin her credit. Have you ever had that happen to you? Can you see how frustrating it would be to know you're in the right and not be able to prove it?

6. Lindy's late husband, Ben, was a white-colla criminal. She assumes that others in the com munity see her as just as guilty as Ben was. I it human nature to spread the blame like that

7. As Lindy begins working for Thad at Pear son Products, her son seems to become more settled, too. Have you ever noticed how one family member's mood can affect everyone— either positively or negatively?

8. Thad teaches Sunday school to help himsel feel as if he's making amends to children, in cluding his brother's orphaned kids. Is tha logical? Will it really do him good?

9. Lindy's return to church is hard for her afte having been away for months. Do you go to church? Why or why not? Are you waiting fo someone to ask you? (If you're waiting for the congregation to become perfect first it migh be a long wait!)

10. The CASA representatives in my stories are just regular folks who care deeply about chil dren. Have you ever known someone who vol unteered like this? Could you do it? Why o why not?

11. The town of Serenity has both a regular police force and a county sheriff. Do you think the officers in such a small community would have the kind of success that city cops do? A hint: the police where I live, in the rural Ozarks, solve an amazing number of crimes.

12. During times of danger and upheaval, many townspeople gather to watch what's happening, such as when smoke pours from the jail. Is that what you'd do? Would you be ready to help if asked?

13. When Thad figures out that there are more factions after Lindy than they had thought, he puts his life on the line to save her. Isn't that totally in character for a man who was a dedicated marine?

14. In the Bible, money isn't called the root of all evil. Did you know that? It's "the love of money" that causes the problems (I Timothy 6:10). Can you see why James Reed was willing to sacrifice everything?

15. I waited until Lindy and Thad had confessed their love for each other before mentioning that they had earned a big reward. That wasn't an accident. Do you know people who thought

LARGER-PRINT BOOKS!

GET 2 FREE LARGER-PRINT NOVELS PLUS 2 FREE MYSTERY GIFTS

Love Inspired
SUSPENSE
RIVETING INSPIRATIONAL ROMANCE

Larger-print novels are now available...

LARGER-PRINT BOOKS!

**GET 2 FREE
LARGER-PRINT NOVELS
PLUS 2 FREE
MYSTERY GIFTS**

Love Inspired

Larger-print novels are now available...